MOSES
IN EGYPT

MOSES
IN EGYPT

A novel inspired by
THE PRINCE OF EGYPT
and
THE BOOK OF EXODUS

BY LYNNE REID BANKS

DREAMWORKS

For Kristin Gilson

PUFFIN BOOKS
Published by the Penguin Group
Penguin Putnam Books for Young Readers, 345 Hudson Street,
New York, New York 10014, U.S.A.
Penguin Books Ltd, 27 Wrights Lane, London W8 5TZ, England
Penguin Books Australia Ltd, Ringwood, Victoria, Australia
Penguin Books Canada Ltd, 10 Alcorn Avenue, Toronto,
Ontario, Canada M4V 3B2
Penguin Books (N.Z.) Ltd, 182-190 Wairau Road, Auckland 10, New Zealand

Penguin Books Ltd, Registered Offices: Harmondsworth, Middlesex, England

First published in the United States of America by Puffin Books,
a member of Penguin Putnam Books for Young Readers, 1998

1 3 5 7 9 10 8 6 4 2

ISBN 0-14-130217-8

Printed in the United States of America

CONTENTS

A note about this book:

The story of Moses is among the most powerful and
enduring stories of all time. It is revered by the world's
three major religions, and has been retold in many
different versions throughout history and around the
world.

This literary adaptation of the story of Moses is
written by Lynne Reid Banks, a renowned author of
books for children. It is a novel inspired by the motion
picture *The Prince of Egypt,* and by the biblical text on
which that motion picture is based.

In creating the story of *The Prince of Egypt,* certain historical and artistic license was taken. Such
creative liberties have been taken here as well. This
novel is not intended to be identical to the film in all
matters of character, dialogue, and themes, nor is it
intended to be a literal depiction of the biblical story.
The author brings her own artistic vision to the work,
and has used this vision to develop her own interpre-
tation of the story.

The biblical retelling of the story of Moses can be
found in the Book of Exodus.

PART ONE

CHAPTER 1

THE BABY
IN THE
REEDS

T he little family crouched in their mud-brick hovel and watched the soldiers tramping past, their spears in their hands, full of fell purpose.

The mother, thin and ragged, hugged her youngest child—a boy of three months—sheltering him beneath the ends of her head-scarf. Her other two children, a girl of eight and a boy of four, huddled close to her, utterly silent until the patrol passed.

The little girl, Miriam, then whispered urgently, "They'll be back, *Ima*! We must run—now!"

Yocheved, the mother, trembled with terror. It seemed too dangerous to leave the house. But Miriam was right. On the way back, the patrol might break down their door and find them.

"Give me the basket!" she whispered.

The two children quickly brought from its hiding place a large, round, tight-lidded basket made of woven reeds smeared with pitch. They carried it between them, while Yocheved, clasping the baby close, peered left and right out of the door before leaving the poor shelter of their home and flitting through the narrow alleys of the slave quarters, alert to every sound that might mean the soldiers were returning.

Once clear of the humble buildings, they were in the open. Nothing hid them here. They ran as fast as they could, down the sloping sandbanks to the edge of the River Nile.

There, Miriam handed the basket to her mother.

Now was the moment Yocheved had long dreaded, when she would have to part from her youngest child. Lifting the lid, she gave her baby one last passionate cuddle, and laid it inside, drawing her finger out of the soft, strong grip of the dimpled hand. She gazed at him through a veil of tears. She tried to sing her own lullaby to him once more, but her voice was choked. She could not bear the thought that she might never see him again.

There was no time to delay—the sun was going down. Yocheved waded into the river and set the basket afloat. They had tested its buoyancy many times, using stone weights instead of the baby. It would float; it would carry its precious burden downriver on its voyage—to death or destiny, as God would decide.

There could be no last farewells. The river snatched

the little craft from her clinging hands and carried it away.

"Follow it, Miriam!" said Yocheved to her daughter. Miriam, on shore, began to run, her head turned to keep the basket in sight. The mother stood waist-deep for a few moments, watching her treasure borne away. Then with a heavy sigh, she regained dry land, lifted Aaron on to her hip and went home. To weep, and wait.

It was just as well she did not see the hazards that the basket had to pass through. They were more than a mother's heart could have endured.

But the child Miriam was witness to everything. A helpless witness; for what could she do but watch in breath-stopped horror as the dreadful saw-toothed jaws of a crocodile emerged from the depths and snapped at the basket as it passed? If a hippopotamus had not surged to the surface between them and attacked the attacker, the baby would have made a meal for the brute, as many another had before. Such was the law in the Land of Egypt at that time: babies —certain babies—were crocodiles' lawful prey.

The basket swept on, with Miriam running alongside it on the shore.

A fishing vessel blocked her view as it passed in

the other direction. Her heart was in her mouth as she saw the fishermen fling their wide nets over the side, just where the basket was riding on the bow-wave of the boat. Could they miss drawing it in with their catch? The kindest-hearted of them would not dare to do anything but fling its helpless contents back into the river if they found it.

But the boat passed on its way and Miriam, with relief sharp as a sword-thrust, saw, beyond the stern, that the black oval shape was still there, still safe, still on its destined way.

Now she was level with the Great Palace, where lived the dreaded Pharaoh and his queen. Of all places, the basket must not stop here: it was from Pharaoh's merciless decree against the Hebrews, who were his slaves, that Miriam and her mother were trying to save the little one.

"Go past! Go past!" whispered Miriam, clenching her hands.

But chance, or God's will, ordained otherwise.

There was a semi-circle of reeds here, protruding far out into the river. They enclosed a specially created pool for the queen's pleasure, where crocodiles could not come. Miriam, hands to her mouth, watched the basket floating toward this obstacle. Yes! It would surely pass!

And then she saw one of Pharaoh the king's royal barges rounding a bend in the river. Its great black prow, decorated with a carved lotus flower, was heading straight for the basket! Miriam could see that everything depended on the prow pushing the basket *away* from the palace and the reeds, toward the far bank. She closed her eyes and sent a frantic prayer to God.

"Be good to us! Save him and I will serve You always, and he will do Your will!"

Somehow she felt certain that if God answered this prayer, it would mean not only the saving of her brother's life, but that it should be saved for a purpose.

When she dared to open her eyes, the barge was surging past. But—oh, horror!—the basket was on *her* side, being rapidly pushed in to the circle of papyrus reeds by the swift, churning movements of the oars.

The barge passed out of sight. The basket was stuck fast in the reeds.

Miriam fell face down in the sand, exhausted and despairing. But she roused herself. God must have a reason for this seeming heedlessness. He *must*!

She stood up and glanced around. On the horizon, the sinking sun settled for a few moments, like a great burnished bronze disk she had once seen her face in, in the market. It was as if the sun, too, had paused to watch what happened. Then it shrugged and began to slip down behind the sand hills.

Miriam crept through the reeds until she was crouching near the pool. Dared she enter it and try to free the basket? No, too late! She could hear voices —women's voices, laughing and talking. They were making their way along the private path from the palace.

Tiy, Queen of Egypt, was coming down to the river shore with her women to bathe in the cool of the evening.

She didn't see in the tall papyrus the little girl whose bright, fearful eyes watched her. She was too occupied with herself, the chatter of her women, the calm green-fringed beauty of her pleasure-pool at sunset. And her little boy, who clung to her hand.

While her son played in the shallows, the Queen prepared to enter the river. She kicked off her silver sandals and stood with her feet in the gently lapping water. Two of the women removed her horsehair wig, an elaborate creation like a helmet decorated with golden ornaments. Another carefully took off her gold and enamel earrings, her heavy neckpiece, and her many bracelets shaped like gold snakes coiling around her arms. Then she moved forward into the embrace of the cool water.

She was in up to her waist when she saw it: a strange black thing, caught in the reeds. It didn't belong there, and she gave a little scream. But she calmed herself and, without turning, gave a command.

"Some of you, go and see what that is, and bring it to me!"

Two of her women, fully dressed, instantly entered the river and pushed forward till they reached the black thing. They bent over it, waist-deep in the water.

As they lifted the lid, the Queen instantly knew that it was not just a stray piece of flotsam, but something momentous. She knew it from the way the women straightened, gazing at each other and then, openmouthed, back at her.

"So? What is it?"

"A basket, mistress!"

"I see it's a basket. What's in it?"

For answer, they floated it between them till it rested on the surface of the pool in front of her.

The two women watched breathlessly as the Queen bent to look. A little smile moved her mouth, an instinctive womanly tenderness touched her eyes.

"Sacred Ra, a child!"

She lifted the baby in her arms and held it to her.

Miriam, from her hiding place, could see the familiar strong little hands waving, clutching. She heard him chuckle, as always when he was picked up. She saw his feet, kicking. He was well-fleshed. His mother's milk had made his olive-golden skin smooth and shiny.

"A goodly boy," said the Queen. She laughed aloud now, a motherly, indulgent laugh, and continued to play with him for a moment or two. Then she said, "He must be one of the Hebrew children. And not newborn! Some mother has preserved him by hiding him—I've heard they try to do that, but usually they are found out. Your mother," she said to the baby, "is cleverer than most. Perhaps that means you are clever, too. You have a bright-eyed look. You are smooth as a little fish, and as slippery—you have given the slip to our laws!" She nuzzled him, kissed him, and then remarked with a sigh: "How sad it all is! Slaves love their little ones as we do, it seems. . . . But they bear too many. Too many! Still . . . one more or less can make no difference. What say you, my women, shall we save him?"

They all put up little birdlike cries of agreement, and clapped their delicate hands. Every face was smiling. What a romance! A child from the river, and the Queen pitying him!

Only the little boy, looking up from his play by the river and seeing his mother fondling a baby, felt a pang of unease.

"Wait, though!" said the Queen. "What would Pharaoh say? Oh, but the babe is so sweet. I love him already—but how shall I feed him?"

A wave of fearful excitement passed over the child Miriam. This was her moment!

Daring all, she emerged from the reeds.

"Majesty," Miriam cried out, or tried to cry out, but her throat would not pass the word.

"Great gods! Another little slave from the rushes!"

Miriam stood before her, shaking from head to foot.

"If you take him, Majesty," she whispered, "I will bring a woman to the palace who can nurse him!"

There was an astonished silence. The Queen, holding Miriam's baby brother in her arms, stared at her through her huge, slanting eyes, made bigger by the cunning arts of face painting. It was as if the statue of a goddess confronted Miriam with a gaze that could strike her dead.

"Good," she said abruptly. "This is the will of the gods. It is meant to be. Bring her tonight through the servants' way." Forgetting her bath, she left the river and began to hurry back to the palace, cradling the baby and cooing to him. Then, remembering her own boy, she looked back. He was trotting along after her, an anxious frown on his face.

"Come, Rameses!" she said, with joy in her voice. "Come and meet your new baby brother. We will call him Moses!"

The group receded along the path to the Great Palace. Miriam, watching them, felt a strangeness mingled with her intense relief. Of all the places in the world, this was the last she would have expected to provide sanctuary for her little brother. Yet he had been saved. And here he would grow up as a prince!

As she ran home to tell her mother the wonderful news, the Queen's fateful words were ringing in her brain: *"This is the will of the gods."* Only it was not the Egyptian gods that Miriam believed were at work here, devising a special destiny for her brother.

It was the God of the Hebrews, whom she would never doubt again as long as she lived.

CHAPTER 2

THE YOUNG PRINCES

The Queen, having made up her mind to take the baby to her heart, never wavered further. How she persuaded her husband, the all-mighty Pharaoh, to allow her to keep the small slave-child, was never known. They had but one child of their own, and a man craves more than one son. However it happened, the boy was accepted and treated as a prince of the royal house.

The Queen must, surely she *must*, have known that the woman Miriam brought to the palace that first night was none other than the baby's natural mother. The child recognized her and her breasts flowed with milk for him—the more so when she had had a few days of the rich palace food and had put on flesh. He seemed to know her songs.

One in particular, the Queen noted, always calmed the child. A little jealous, she tried to learn it to sing it to him herself, but the words and the tune eluded her. Little did she know how simple it was in Hebrew:

> *"Hush now, my baby.*
> *Be still, love, don't cry.*
> *Sleep as you're rocked by the stream.*
> *Sleep and remember*
> *My last lullaby*
> *So I'll be with you when you dream."*

Yocheved sometimes took Miriam with her on her regular visits to the palace, and she was accepted as part of the household. The servants petted and indulged her.

She tasted for the first time all sorts of delicious, exotic foods and nectarous drinks. Amazed by the plenty and the splendor, and feeling guilty to be enjoying it alone, she would hide little pastries filled with green nuts and dripping with honey under her clothes to take home to her brother Aaron.

The family lived in a district apart from the Egyptian city, called Goshen. It was a place of acute poverty, of tents, huts, and hovels of mud bricks, open to the sky or roofed with straw. The contrast with the palace could not have been more extreme.

Miriam had work to do around her family's hut,

more than ever since her mother spent time at the palace. But she didn't mind. Her sense of her destiny grew. She couldn't have explained it in words, but she felt it strongly. Something to do with *him*— with Moses.

The Queen had named him with a name often used by Egyptians, with the addition of a god's name —Ra-Moses, Tut-Moses. But Moses, plain Moses, came also from a Hebrew word that meant "to draw out." *Out of the water.* Had the Queen known that? Of course not. She knew not a single word of the slave-tongue. His naming was, Miriam decided, part of the wondrous pattern in which she so strongly believed.

When the boy was a little less than three years old, he was weaned, and Yocheved was casually sent away. Miriam also. Yocheved sang her loving lullaby to the toddler one last time, and then, sad but satisfied, she and her daughter went back to their lives as part of the slave community in Goshen.

But even then, Miriam found ways to follow Moses' fortunes as the years passed.

Moses grew to boyhood beside Rameses, the Queen's own son. Miriam still occasionally saw them on their outings in the town, and her old friends among the palace servants kept her informed. So she retained a secret link with these princelings, loving only one of them but paying respect to both.

Clinging steadfastly to her belief that Moses had some great destiny, she was puzzled by the fact that *he* seemed quite unaware of it. Like his older brother, he was a harum-scarum, loudmouthed, mischievous, willful youth. Truly a young prince, spoiled with luxurious living, rich food, fine linen, priceless body ornaments, with servants to minister to his every need. He had horses to ride and child-sized weapons to play with, an all-powerful ruler for a father, and an adoring queen for a mother. Not a hand's turn of work did either of the boys do until they were grown.

Of course they had many things to learn, but their tutors—two high priests of the temple called Huy and Hotep—dared not insist if their pupils grew bored, or ran away from their lessons. Only a stern word from the Pharaoh (to whom the priests were obliged to give truthful reports of the boys' progress) would force them back to the schoolroom.

There they learned mathematics, astrology, and the complex history of Egypt and its pharaonic dynasties, which stretched back over two thousand years. They learned to engrave pictograms, write and paint on papyrus, and impress hieroglyphics into clay tablets.

Rameses, who was his father's heir, had to learn much about the skills of government. They also studied music, art, and declamation. Most vital of all, they had to learn the names and functions of the many gods and how they must be served.

But their favorite lessons took place in the stables and on the shore of the Nile below the palace, where they practiced spear-throwing and swordsmanship, archery, riding, and chariot-driving.

Thus their childhood passed pleasantly enough, while beyond the palace grounds many things took place that they knew about, and even saw, but never thought of. They were simply part of the order of things, from which they drew great benefit and in which they were encouraged to take pride.

Huge building projects were constantly in progress, and sometimes their father, Seti the Pharaoh, took them to inspect his great works. These were to last forever, and make Seti's name renowned—if possible, more so than former pharaohs' had been before him.

The boys saw, and yet did not see, the masses of wretched slaves toiling in the brick fields and quarries and on the building sites. They saw the overseers beating them. They heard their cries and saw them dropping with exhaustion. And they noticed nothing. Nothing but the steady, magnificent rising, higher and higher above the desert sands, of the great monuments ordered and designed by their all-powerful father.

Like any brothers, the boys were as often rivals as friends. Whatever mischief there was to get into, Moses led the way. As the younger son, he was the most headstrong and the least burdened by responsibility. Rameses was stubborn and changeable, quick of temper, easily cast down and as easily uplifted. Moses' nature was deeper; he was more watchful, slower to rouse—but once roused, nothing but victory would satisfy him.

Miriam thought of him as like the Nile, his surface glitteringly reflecting sun, moon, and stars, but (she firmly believed) with hidden depths and currents no one could sound. Rameses was like the cataracts higher up the river, tumultuous, dashing, uncontrolled. The servants were afraid of Rameses, who often had them flogged; but they were more respectful of Moses, who had a way of reproving them with a look. They sensed something in him, something alien. "He's not like us," they would say. And they whispered among themselves about his origins.

Moses knew nothing of this. He had no reason to suppose he was not a true son of the royal house. Everything he had, everything around him, lulled him, and conspired to make him question nothing, certainly not the great cruelties that underpinned the life of his family. He took it all for granted.

Miriam held her love for her natural brother in her heart and wondered what holy purpose lay behind this strange adoption. There was only one thing she could think of, and gradually she became certain that it was for *this* that Moses had been redeemed: so that he might become a redeemer. A redeemer of his suffering people. But how was he ever to learn that they *were* his people?

When Miriam thought about this, she could not see how it could come about. Yet in her prayers she laid her bold dream at God's feet and built an unshakable faith upon it.

CHAPTER 3

THE CHARIOT RACE

One day when the boys were nearly men, and had acquired men's skills, they quarreled over some trifle. Moses challenged Rameses to a chariot race to decide the matter.

They rushed to the stables and each ordered two fine, fast horses to be harnessed to two small but beautifully crafted chariots made of wood and iron coated in gold. Side by side, taunting each other, they drove out through the rear gates of the palace. There they put on speed, urging their horses into swift gallops so that their small hooves hardly seemed to stir the dust, though the wheels of the lightweight chariots threw fountains of sand behind them.

The young princes were soon driving like mad-men. Moses kept his eyes on the road between his horses' ears, but he was acutely aware of Rameses just ahead of him.

At a turn in the road beside a temple wall, Moses saw his opportunity.

"Hey, brother, how would you like your face carved on a wall?"

"Some day, yes!"

"Why not now?"

Moses swerved his chariot so that its wheel struck his brother's chariot. It glanced off the wall, giving Rameses a jolt. He tried to retaliate, but Moses pulled his horse back and Rameses shot past him off the road and down a slope. The chariot tilted and nearly overturned.

Rameses pulled up, breathing hard. He stared around him. "Moses?" he yelled. Nothing. . . . Then, suddenly, Moses' chariot appeared at the top of the slope.

"You called?" he shouted cheerfully, and before Rameses could reply, the horses were hurtling down the slope heading straight for him. Scared, Rameses lashed his pair, which reared up and then plunged forward with Moses giving chase.

They raced through a sector of the town at full gallop, scattering market stalls to left and right. At one point they even raced down a flight of shallow steps. Two old men playing backgammon in a square leapt aside just in time as the two princes crashed through their table, scattering the gaming pieces.

"Heedless young scallywags!" muttered one, as they scrambled from the dust and tried to recover from their fright and collect their game.

The "scallywags" had meanwhile passed through the town and reached a construction site. The monument in its midst was a temple surmounted by a gigantic head of Seti, their father. As was the custom among the pharaohs of Egypt, this was being erected on his orders as part of his memorial, well in advance of his death. It was of great importance to him, so it was unfortunate that the headstrong young princes' random course had brought them to this of all places.

But they were too blind with the excitement of the chase to notice where they were. Rameses drove his chariot at full gallop up a ramp used for transporting blocks on wooden rollers to the top of the unfinished monument. Moses followed. A group of slaves who were dragging a load upward skidded and slipped on the rollers and the load of blocks fell fifty cubits to the ground. Both boys let out heartless whoops of laughter and drove on.

Rounding a bend in the ramp at full speed, they encountered another workman, halfway up a ladder leaning against the cheek of the statue. As the luckless man took a flying leap to save himself, the ladder knocked against the statue's mighty nose, recently fitted and not yet secured. It broke off and fell, narrowly missing Rameses as he hurtled past below. It bounced off the ramp and landed at the feet of Huy and Hotep, the princes' tutors and high priests of the palace temple, who were standing on the ground, gaping upward in dismay.

The nose smashed. Pieces of it flew in all directions, striking the startled priests and sending them running. But worse was to come. As the priests fled past an immense wooden structure like a dam, the young princes, who had descended by another ramp, passed by at top speed. First one and then another of the props that upheld the barrier were knocked away by the spinning chariot wheels.

The princes, happily unaware, flew on, still lashing their foaming horses and shouting cheerful insults at each other. But in their wake there was a moment's pause, an ominous creaking, and then a gathering rumble.

"Aaaagh! Look out—"

The vast wooden wall slowly fell, and from behind it the tons of loose sand that it had been holding back descended upon the priests in a mighty avalanche.

It took all of an hour to dig the priests out, and although miraculously they were unhurt, their dignity was badly damaged.

When they emerged, hawking and spitting the sand from their throats, shaking it from their robes and wiping it from their eyes, they saw a scene of devastation. Every part of the temple that had been finished had been either brought crashing to the ground or buried in sand. It would be months before the damage could be made good.

The priests looked from the wreckage to each other.

"They have gone too far this time," said the one called Huy, with a certain grim relish. "This time the Pharaoh must act."

"Have no fear," said Hotep. "This time it was *his memorial.*"

They looked up at their noseless Pharaoh and almost saw the funny side. Almost, but not quite, although quite a lot of the men who had dug them out did.

The young miscreants had only the faintest feelings of unease when they finished their race in a draw, handed over their sweat-lathered horses to the grooms, and, with their arms around each other's shoulders, made their unsuspecting way back to the palace.

But their laughter died in their throats when they were summoned to their father's presence.

Even though they were accustomed to luxury, the

magnificence of Seti's chamber, where he kept his state, was daunting. It was a hall whose high ceiling was supported by stone pillars, carved to imitate columns of papyrus, with lotus capitols. The walls, built of huge blocks of dressed stone, were covered in paintings and incised carvings of great splendor and exquisite coloration, depicting the gods and scenes of triumph from Seti's, and earlier pharaohs', reigns. There was a minimum of furniture, though of the utmost beauty and luxury, giving an overall impression of space and grandeur.

The young princes advanced with care across the polished marble floor. It seemed to take a very long time to reach the stern figure with folded arms at the far end. They were dismayed to see their tutors, Huy and Hotep, lurking in the background. Their mother was there, too. Was there hope in that? She sometimes took their side.

The youths made their humblest obeisances, but to no avail.

"Why do the gods torment me with such reckless, destructive, blasphemous sons?" their father inquired in tones that chilled their blood. They dared not look at each other. This was to be no ordinary reproof.

Rameses tried to speak, but Seti shouted: "Be still! Your pharaoh speaks! I seek to build an empire, and your only thought is to amuse yourselves by tearing it down. Have I taught you nothing?"

Hotep stepped forward, and said in a voice that the boys thought repulsively oily: "You mustn't be so hard on yourself, Your Majesty. You are an excellent teacher."

"It is not your fault, Great One," chimed Huy, "that your sons have learned—nothing."

"Well, they've learned blasphemy," murmured Hotep behind his hand.

"True . . ."

"Get out!" roared the Pharaoh.

The priests, one tall, one short, slunk away, their rear views making a picture so ridiculous that the boys could have laughed. But one glance at Seti's furious features stifled all mirth.

Moses knew their father's anger would fall heaviest on Rameses as his heir. He mustered his courage and stepped forward. "Father. The fault is mine. I goaded Rameses on to race, so I am responsible."

"Responsible? I wonder if either of you knows the meaning of the word!"

"I understand, Father—" began the unhappy Rameses.

"And do you also understand the task for which your birth has destined you? Have you comprehended the ancient traditions that you must maintain, *and build upon*? When I travel into the next world, the burden of leadership will pass to you. Do you think yourself fit to guide the destiny of our great nation, to be bowed down to and obeyed, to be called the Morning and Evening Star?"

"One damaged temple—" began Rameses under his breath.

"Speak up, boy!"

Rameses' head came up and he spoke defiantly. "One damaged temple does not destroy centuries of tradition!"

Seti looked at him with his black eyes narrowed. He pinioned his son with those eyes until the boy could no longer meet them.

"But *one weak link* can break the chain of a mighty dynasty," Seti said with deathly quietness.

There was a terrible silence in the great hall. Moses glanced under his eyelashes at his brother and was astonished to see that he had broken out into a sudden sweat.

The Queen glided forward and laid a restraining hand on her husband's arm. Seti relaxed fractionally.

"You have my leave to go," he said coldly.

Rameses drew a sharp breath, as if about to speak. Then he bowed and left the chamber.

Moses felt his brother's humiliation and pain. Instead of following, as was his place, he faced the Pharaoh.

"Father, it was my fault."

"How?"

"I did challenge him. I did keep the race going. I did lead the way to the temple."

"But Rameses was first up the ramp."

"He was winning," said Moses craftily.

He thought he saw a faint smile pass over Seti's face, but it was quickly erased.

"Moses, you will never have to carry such a burden as the crown—the double crown of Upper and Lower Egypt—that I will pass to Rameses. He must not allow himself to be led astray. Not even by you, my son."

"He yearns for your approval. If you could bring yourself to show that you trust him, he won't disappoint you. He needs only the opportunity to prove himself."

There was a silence that Moses couldn't interpret. He knew he had taken a great risk in pleading like this. But the Queen was smiling and nodding gently. At last, his father put a hand on his shoulder.

"I shall consider what you have said. Go now. I shall see you both tonight at my banquet."

CHAPTER 4

THE MIDIANITE

Moses went in search of his brother, and found him quite quickly. He had taken refuge on the lap of a great statue where they often came to find privacy. The vast size of the statue somehow gave them reassurance; also, it housed Horus, the falcon-headed god to whom one could pray for forgiveness and comfort. Moses climbed up beside Rameses.

"Let's play a trick on those tale-bearing priests," Moses suggested.

There was no reply. Rameses' head was sunk between his shoulders.

"They're coming this way. Look—I brought a water-sack. We can drop it on their heads." Silence. "I happen to know that Hotep has a new robe. Wouldn't it be some relief to soak it for him?"

"It would be childish."

"Oho!" teased Moses. "So we have grown up, have we, in the last few painful hours?"

"Perhaps it's time *we* did. Though I see no signs of it in your case."

"Ssssh! Here they come!"

Moses leaned over. He could see the two men, heads bent in conversation, approaching along the path below. Rameses' remark about growing up almost made him change his mind about his prank, but when he heard the priests chuckling together, it maddened him. He held the water bag out to the length of his arm, and at a strategic moment, let it fall, then quickly ducked down, out of sight.

His aim was excellent. There was a pause, then a loud splash, followed by gasps and furious exclamations.

"Oh! My new robe!"

"You'll be in trouble for this, you young scoundrel—be sure of it!"

Moses knew that only Rameses was visible, and quaked with laughter that his brother was taking the blame. He imagined the white faces and shaken fists, and rolled gleefully on his back between the statue's massive knees. As the priests made off, still calling back threats, Moses kicked his legs in the air, laughing so hard it took time to notice that Rameses was not sharing the joke.

"Why aren't you laughing? Surely you can see they deserved it!"

"But did I deserve my father's words? They hurt me, Moses!"

"Which ones? He said so many!"

"The weak link. He said I was the weak link." He turned an anguished face to Moses in the moonlight. "Moses, you've sat by me in history lessons. You know how many thousands of years our Egyptian empire has lasted. There have been strong pharaohs and weak ones; pharaohs who conquered and those who were conquered, those who traded and built our great institutions and monuments—and those who were lazy and weak, and let them slip away."

"Only to be built up again."

"But with what an effort! Hundreds of times greater than the effort it will take to rebuild that temple we damaged today. It can take a whole long reign, even a whole dynasty, to rebuild what a 'weak link' lets be destroyed."

"Oh, come on, brother! You're not going to be that sort of pharaoh."

"My father thinks I might. He said so. Am I to be the one who lets it all go?"

Moses stood up and stretched. "Oh, yes, I'm sure you will! During the reign of Rameses the Second, temples will crash and crumble back into the dunes. Tombs will be broken into and their treasures stolen. The Nubians will invade and conquer, the Syrians will overrun what's left, the Hittite barbarians will carry us all into slavery. Why, I wouldn't wonder if there was even an uprising of the Hebrew slaves! Single-handedly, you'll bring the greatest kingdom on earth to ruin!"

But Rameses did not reward him with a smile. "Don't mock such an awful possibility," he said quietly. "The gods may be listening."

"I'll tell you what will make the gods prick up their sacred ears," said Moses drily. "The uproar there will be if we're late for the banquet."

Rameses leapt to his feet.

"Great Thoth! I forgot all about it!"

They raced each other back to the palace and ran to the banqueting hall, where they lurked outside the great golden doors for a moment or two, afraid to enter.

"Father will eviscerate me," muttered Rameses.

"I'll see you get a magnificent sarcophagus," said Moses. "Come on. Nobody will even notice us coming in."

Mustering their courage, they opened one of the doors just wide enough to slip through. Then they stopped. To their horror they found that a platform had been built just inside the doors, on which was a long table laden with golden dishes, jeweled goblets, centerpieces of scented lotus blossoms, and a feast of exotic food. Seated with their backs to them were their royal parents and other dignitaries; and beyond, in the body of the great hall, hundreds of noble guests.

The moment they were spotted, the entire hall seemed to erupt in cheers and applause. Their parents' backs turned into faces, and the boys, dazed, realized they were the focus of every eye.

"Nobody will notice—eh?" muttered Rameses out of the corner of his mouth to Moses. "Only everyone who is anyone in the entire city!"

But their mother was beckoning to them. And she was smiling! They came forward, hot with shame, and Rameses was astonished to be greeted with a warm hug.

"My boy," she whispered urgently. "Your father has just named you Prince Regent!"

"What!"

"You are now responsible for overseeing all the temples."

Rameses stood speechless while the banqueters roared approval.

"Go and thank your father," the Queen prompted through the uproar.

Rameses obeyed her as if in a trance. The Queen turned to Moses.

"Apparently Pharaoh thought he *only needed the opportunity,*" she said with a twinkle in her eye.

Moses watched father and son embracing. He was not envious. The task before his brother was daunting—Moses had no ambition for such a burden of responsibility. Overseeing all the temple-building! Phew! Well, in a sense that was a case of the punishment—or the reward—exactly fitting the crime. There would be no more reckless chariot-racing now. This was indeed the beginning of being grown-up.

Just then Moses saw the two high priests enter by a side door. They had changed their wet garments but their faces were still full of anger. A mischievous notion came to him.

"My Lord Pharaoh," Moses said respectfully, as the hubbub below died down and he could be heard, "I propose that the High Priests offer tribute to their new regent."

"An excellent idea!" replied Seti. "And here they are! What fitting tribute can you offer, holy ones?"

Hotep and Huy glared at Moses, but were forced to obey. They bowed, and while bowing exchanged a few muttered words.

"Majesty," said Hotep smoothly. "A raiding party has brought back a tender prize stolen from the Midianites, one of the desert tribes. May we offer it to Lord Rameses?"

A smile lit up the Pharaoh's face.

"Let us inspect this—prize," he said. "We will judge its worthiness."

There followed some hocus-pocus, in which Huy and Hotep—who, like all Egyptian priests, were also magicians—were skilled. The crowd were collected near an artificial pool in the center of the banqueting hall; there were some bursts of flame and a mysterious, colored smoke screen, and with a flourish Hotep announced the offering of a "delicate desert flower."

Through the smoke appeared Huy, leading a camel on which sat a veiled, but evidently extremely angry, young woman, her arms bound.

There was no time to examine her or judge her beauty. Her struggles against her bonds dislodged her from the beast's back, and Moses, seeing her slipping, instinctively rushed to break her fall. He was rewarded by a sharp kick, and retreated hastily while the crowd tried to suppress laughter. Here was a spirited "prize" indeed! The eyes of all the men glistened, and Huy, whose idea this had been, grinned at the success of his gift.

His happiness was short-lived. The girl had jumped to her feet, and by throwing her weight against the rope, pulled Huy off his. A roar of laughter went up as he landed hard on his stomach. She began to drag him along the floor as she made a futile effort to run away. Hotep joined his colleague on the end of the rope, but such was the little hoyden's strength that she managed to drag them both along for a short distance, the crowd, highly entertained, giving way before her.

"Come along, my son!" said Pharaoh. "Are you going to allow your 'prize' to escape, taking my high priests with her back to her desert tent?"

Rameses nimbly jumped in front of the girl and put up his hand to stop her. Moving her head as swiftly as any striking cobra, she bit him right through her veil.

The crowd's laughter died in a gasp. To attack the prince was an act of treason. The dismayed priests, now on their feet, dragged her back. But Rameses, sucking his bitten hand, made light of it.

"More of a desert snake than a desert flower," he said with a wry smile, to show that he was not truly angry.

"And you are no snake charmer," joked Moses.

"True. That's why I'm giving her to you," retorted Rameses. He snatched the rope from Hotep and handed it to Moses with a flourish.

Moses stood still. He looked from his brother to the struggling girl. Then he stepped up to her and pulled the veil from her face—and froze.

She was the loveliest thing he had ever seen.

For a brief second they stared into each other's eyes. Then she hissed: "I will not be given to anyone! Especially an arrogant, pampered palace brat!"

Now the crowd was truly shocked. A wild creature, trapped, may be forgiven for frantic, animal behavior. But a verbal insult! A waiting hush fell upon the room.

"Well, brother? What have you to say to that?" Rameses asked.

Moses, confused and offended, stood before the beautiful angry girl and tried to show resolution.

"You will pay proper respect to a prince of Egypt."

"I am paying you the respect you deserve—none!" she replied. And spat in his face.

Now the crowd fell back, appalled at what amounted to blasphemy, for the royal family were demigods. The girl tried to make a dash for freedom, but Moses gripped the rope.

"Be still!" he ordered. She backed away. He made the rope taut, trying to haul her toward him. But she pulled and pulled in a frenzy.

Moses knew he must do something to defuse a situation that could quite easily end in the girl's death. As she backed toward the pool, he saw his opportunity.

"Let me go!" she shrieked, pulling desperately and throwing her head back as if she heard freedom calling and could not reach it.

"As you wish," said Moses, and let go the rope.

Off-balance, the girl fell backwards into the pool with a great splash.

The tension broke like a wand. The entire crowd broke into roars of laughter. Even the priests, though dismayed, smiled sourly. But Moses was suddenly stricken with fear—her arms were tied. Desert people cannot swim and the water was quite deep enough to drown in.

"Fish her out, Hotep," he said.

"Me, Your Highness?"

"Yes, you! And be quick about it!" Moses suddenly roared.

But Hotep had been wet through once that evening. He merely took the rope, dragged the spluttering girl to the edge of the pool and let her clamber out by herself.

"I shall be revenged! My father will avenge me!" she sobbed. She was frightened and in tears from her ducking, but she still had enough spirit for defiance.

Her garments clung to her lithe body and her long black hair dripped down her face. Moses could not take his eyes off her.

Rameses called to a servant. "Get her dried off and take her to Prince Moses' chamber!"

The girl was bundled away. Moses drew a deep breath and tried to relieve the strange pressure in his chest. The Queen came up to him and wiped the spittle off his face with a square of fine linen.

"Little vixen, how dared she!" she said, loudly enough to be heard by those nearest. But then she leaned toward Moses. "Poor little thing," she murmured, for his ears alone. "I liked her spirit. Men can be so cruel, Moses. Treat her gently."

Moses felt the blush rise up his face and under his heavy wig.

Rameses was saying something to their father. Moses, overcome with a strange confusion, suddenly heard his own name.

"If it pleases you, Father, my first act as Regent is to appoint Prince Moses as Royal Chief Architect."

Moses drew in his breath. He felt his hand seized, and the next moment a heavy ring was pushed onto his finger.

He looked down at it. It was a beautiful smooth emerald in a heavy gold setting. The two boys hugged each other, elated by the coming of manhood. Moses forgot everything for the moment in a wave of gratitude to his brother for sharing his moment of triumph.

"Come, let us resume the banquet! The entertainment is over," said the Pharaoh, and the royal family and their many guests went back to their tables and began to feast.

Only Moses, thinking of what was awaiting him in his chambers, found his throat closed against anything as commonplace as food.

CHAPTER 5

REVELATION
AT THE
WELL

fter the feast, to much teasing from his father and brother, Moses took leave of his family and made his way through the quiet palace to his own apartment.

He did not know quite how he felt about the coming encounter with the Midianite. She would be his first woman, and it was time for that, but still he felt unready. He wished she had been the usual thing, some little slave girl for whom he need feel nothing but casual desire. He tried, as he approached his door, to feel nothing but that now, but somehow it was too late. Something had passed between this girl and him that could not be wiped away by wishing.

Perhaps it could not be wiped away at all.

But that was too fearful a thought. He had heard of men trapped by women into a sort of slavery. The fierce beating of his heart, the trembling of his limbs, the sense of something absolutely momentous about to happen—were these the early symptoms of love? No. No! He would not allow himself to fall into anything so—so unsuitable. Defiant, dazzling, and full of spirit as she was, she was still nothing but a captured tribeswoman.

He flung open his door.

Sitting on the bed behind the gauzy net curtain that protected him at night from flying insects was a shape, as softly curved as sand dunes after the wind has smoothed them. He closed the distance between himself and the bed as if pushed from behind, and snatched aside the drape.

There lay not a voluptuous maiden, but the serving man, bound and gagged, eyeing him piteously.

Moses stared at him for five seconds and then rushed to the window.

Down below in the courtyard, lit by the waning moon, he saw a shadowy figure—no, two. One was the girl. The other made Moses doubt his senses. Now how in the name of Nut, who held up the sky, had she managed to find her way to the stables and collect her camel? His admiration for her grew. But he could not let her escape, for all that.

Out in the darkness, Moses turned this way and that, hunting for sight or sound of the runaways. He thought he saw a shadow on a wall some distance away, and at that moment, two guards challenged him. When they saw who it was, they lowered their spears and bowed.

Moses felt his arm raise itself to point to the shadow, which had stopped moving as if frozen to the wall behind the guards. His mouth opened on an order. But instead of giving it, he heard himself say, "There is a man tied up in my bedchamber. Go and release him."

The guards hurried away. Moses looked for the shadow, but it, too, was gone.

"Idiot!" he abused himself. "What did you do that for? Do you want her or don't you?" Before any true answer could form itself in his head, he forced one, the one Rameses would have given. "Of course you do! Besides, prisoners cannot be allowed to escape. Now. Brain, not brawn!" he advised himself, calming his temper. "She is on her way home. Home is some sordid camp in the midst of the desert. She and her camel—Osiris take it!—need water to cross the sands."

He thought of the nearest well, in the next open square. No. She would not stop there—too close to the palace. The Midianites were said to camp to the east, on the side of the city where the Hebrew slaves had their shack-town, what did they call it? Goshen. Yes, she would go that way, guided by the stars.

He unclenched his hands and ran swiftly.

At the place where the slums of the Egyptian city bordered the slums of Goshen, he paused. Yes, he could smell water—the slaves often came to the wells at night because they worked all day. In fact he could hear faint splashings. He moved cautiously forward, and then, hiding behind a wall, he peered out.

In a small open space amid the low, humble dwellings, he saw a little group around a well. The moonlight showed him a man and two women. And a camel! His heart bounded. He had reasoned aright. There she was!

But now he saw that he was almost too late. The camel had already drunk its fill, enough to carry it through days of travel. The girl had slipped the thongs of a water bag over the pommel of the saddle. The man was just boosting her onto its back. The other woman called something softly—some word of farewell in the Hebrew tongue—and before Moses could act, the girl had cried *"Hut-hut!"* and the camel started forward in a fast trot.

Moses leapt forth and gave chase. "Stop!" he shouted. "Stop! I command you!"

Startled, the girl looked back, then struck the camel

on the rump with a stick. It seemed to bound out of its sedate trot into a clumsy gallop. In a moment, they had disappeared into the dark alleys of Goshen. Gone! He had lost her! Why did that make him feel so desolate— and at the same time, so relieved? *She was free....*

He arrived at the well, trying to resolve his mixed feelings into simple anger. The other woman, and the man with her, cringed back from him. The woman saw his garments and said something to the man in a tone of wonder. Then she dropped the water pot she was holding and fell onto her face before Moses.

"Moses!" she said.

She did not say Prince Moses.

"You know me?"

"I know you."

He barely glanced at her. He was still staring after that girl he would never see again, and never be the same for having seen.

"Moses," the woman said again, in a voice full of tenderness and relief. "You have come at last."

He looked down at her now. Her face was raised. He could not see her very clearly but there was some- thing about her that focused his attention. He seemed to recognize her . . . somehow. And she was looking at him—inappropriately. With more than respect and fear. With—rapture.

"What do you mean, slave?" he asked curtly.

"I have waited. I knew you would come."

"What are you talking about?"

Now the man stepped forward. Even in the moonlight, Moses could see that he was her brother. He lifted her brusquely to her feet and muttered to her in Hebrew. He tried to draw her away, but she broke free and came back. She stood before Moses—far too close to him. He had never been so close to a slave. He could smell her poverty and it frightened him.

"I knew you cared about our freedom."

"Your freedom? What can a slave know of freedom?"

"Freedom is all we dream of."

"Why should I care for your dreams?"

He was wondering why he was troubling to talk to her at all, when she electrified him by saying, "Because you are our brother."

He stiffened. By putting herself on his level with such a saying, she had condemned herself to a flogging. Moses did not know what to do. But the other man did.

He grasped his sister and lifted her off her feet.

"My good prince," spluttered the man. "She's exhausted from the day's work. Oh—not that it was too much, we quite enjoyed it," he said fawningly.

"But she's confused and knows not to whom she's speaking."

"I know very well!" cried the woman. "Who better than a sister to know her own brother?"

Moses was aghast. Was this madwoman courting the lash?

"You are no prince of Egypt!" she panted.

"Miriam!" gasped the man who was struggling to restrain her.

"What did you say?" asked Moses, hushed by her recklessness.

"You were born of my mother, Yocheved!"

"I—born of a slave? You must be tired of life to say so!" Moses choked out, almost beside himself with rage.

"You are our brother whom we saved from certain death! We saved you so that you may save us!"

There was a moment's profound silence. Then the man picked the woman up, his hand over her mouth.

"She is ill, Your Highness. Forgive her, I implore you!" He was backing away, half-carrying his sister, stifling her speech. But with a tremendous effort, she wrested herself free.

"Let me go, Aaron! I must tell him now. The basket the Queen keeps in her closet!"

Moses had no notion what she was talking about.

A basket? He had never seen any basket (but then he had never seen inside his mother's closet). This was some wild flight of fancy. But threats seemed to be the only way to stop this woman's voice.

"You shall be punished!"

"I made that basket! You were in it, we put you there, we floated you down the river so that you might be saved!"

"Saved? Saved from what?"

"Ask the man you call Father!"

Moses had to take a moment to recover his speech. Then he exploded.

"How dare you!"

"God saved you to be our deliverer!"

"Enough!"

For a moment she stopped struggling with the man—who released her out of shock—and stood tall and still.

"You are to deliver us out of bondage."

Moses seized her arm and forced her to the ground. If he could have forced her right into it, deep, and covered her with a slab of stone, he would have done it.

"You will regret this night," he snarled, his brain in ferment. *His sister!* This ragged wretch that some rabid dog had bitten! He spun round on his heel and

began to stride back the way he had come, shaking
in every limb, determined to mark his way back and
to send guards here tomorrow to arrest this insuffer-
able woman, and the brother, too, who could not
control her.

And then he stopped.

Because something followed him. Not a missile
thrown at his head as he retreated, but something
stronger. Like a net, like a lash, flicked around his
throat to hold him. An unbreakable filament of
sound.

"Hush now, my baby.
Be still, love, don't cry.
Sleep as you're rocked by the stream.
Sleep and remember
My last lullaby
So I'll be with you when you dream."

For a timeless moment, he was as still as if he had
died and become his own memorial statue. The little
tune entered into him and burrowed like a worm
until it found its place in his buried childhood. There
it nestled with the deep memory of the many many
times he had heard it before, from a woman not
Tiy the Queen, not his mother. He caught flashing

glimpses of *another*—her dark curly hair, her soft bosom, her tender hands, her yearning black eyes. *Like the eyes of the woman by the well.*

Tears sprang uncontrollably to his own eyes. He wrenched himself out of his trance and ran, stumbling, sobbing, back to the palace.

CHAPTER 6

HORROR

Moses did not return directly to his own apartment. Instead he dragged himself through the corridors to the vast room of state where the banquet had been held. He had some dim idea of confronting his parents in the midst of the feast. But it was nearly morning, and the great chamber was empty.

After the departing guests, hundreds of silent servants had passed through the hall like so many locusts, eating up, as it were, every trace of festivity. All was once again clean, spacious, and peaceful. There was not a footmark to mar the gloss of the floor; the pool reflected the pillars and the decorated ceiling, tremorless as a bronze mirror. A few torches burned in sconces around the walls.

Moses stood in the midst of the silent magnificence, his shoulders shaking. He stared around him. *"Ask the man you call Father." "Ask the man you call*

Father." The words beat in his brain, over and over. Yes, he would ask! He was not afraid. He would defeat her foul lies with the sacred truth that his father would tell him.

Yet he did not move.

The scene by the well replayed itself in his mind. The face of the woman called Miriam (why did he remember her name?) was not just any slave's face, to be instantly forgotten. It was as if, like that accursed song, it found an echo in his memory. Yet surely he had never seen her before.

Hush now, my baby. Be still, love, don't cry . . . The words were not Egyptian words, they were in the slave-tongue, a language no highborn Egyptian ever learned. Yet he understood them. He knew their meaning. *Sleep while you're rocked—rocked—*What next? *Rocked by the stream . . .* Why those words? What did they mean? Did they mean what *she* had said? Were they some kind of confirmation of her ludicrous claims?

He sank to the floor beside a pillar and pressed his fists to his throbbing temples. The tune would not leave him; the words spoke themselves in soft insistent whispers, infiltrating his thoughts. He banged his head with his fists till his temples were numb with pain, but they would not go away.

This beautiful palace is my home, he thought

fiercely. *My father—my mother—Rameses—they're my family! I'm part of them! I'm not part of that squalor, those miserable slaves—they're nothing to do with me!* He looked wildly around him. *And all this splendor, all these proofs of a great civilization, are my birthright! They are all I've ever wanted.*

His tortured thoughts forced him into a sort of waking sleep. In this trancelike state, it seemed as if some inner eye opened for the first time, and fastened on the nearest wall, lit by a torch flickering over a painted scene that had slid by his waking eyes a thousand times. Now his very soul focused on it, and it was as if some great unknown power showed it to him for the first time and forced him to truly comprehend it.

It showed the River Nile with crocodiles opening their jaws to receive . . . oh, horror! Little children. Babies, falling headfirst into the water. Not falling. Being thrown . . . Higher on the wall were the throwers. With dread, Moses forced his brain to absorb what he was seeing: Egyptian soldiers of the royal guard. Throwing babies headfirst into the crocodiles' savage jaws. The crocodiles seemed to smile. So did the soldiers.

Moses came to himself and leapt to his feet with a strangled cry. The basket. The basket in his mother's closet. He would seek it there. When it was not there, he would be at peace.

He ran through the silent corridors to the Queen's apartments, and—unprecedentedly, without a knock —burst in.

The Queen was not there. There was no one there but an old servant. She cowered in alarm as he appeared. Moses ignored her. He threw himself against the door of the Queen's great closet and wrenched it. It was locked! Moses turned and addressed the startled old waiting-woman.

"Unfasten this door!" he ordered.

"Your Highness—"

"Do as I bid you!"

The old woman gasped and rushed to obey him. Moses pulled the door out of her hand and flung himself through it.

"Give me light!"

The old woman hurried to fetch a torch, which with trembling hands she set in a sconce.

The closet was large and divided into sections for its varied contents: all the Queen's clothes, her cosmetics, her jewelry, her footwear, her wigs. Moses' eyes were baffled by the mass of shapes and colors. He turned to the pale and trembling waiting-woman.

"Is there a basket here?" It was an absurd question. The closet was full of baskets of all sorts and sizes. But the frightened old woman croaked:

"You—you wish to see the basket, Highness?"

The basket! So there was a basket! He could only nod, his throat suddenly too dry for speech.

The woman reached behind a drape and drew out an old, round, rush basket, covered with pitch. She laid it at his feet and backed away.

Slowly he bent and lifted the lid. He stared into its empty depths.

Then he raised his eyes. The old woman was looking at him. In the torchlight she looked like an ancient tomb-carving of one of the All-Knowing.

"Where—did—this—come—from?" he choked out.

"From the river, Highness," she whispered. "In it the gods sent you to us."

"Do you know this for truth?" His eyes were so terrifying she fell to her knees. "Answer!"

"I was there."

Moses ran like a madman through the palace.

He found his father on a wide balcony overlooking the city, the great monuments—and the river. Moses burst into his presence unannounced just as dawn was breaking. Below them was everything that was great and eternal in Egypt—the pharaonic legacy, Moses' birthright to accept or turn from. But the two men confronted each other as if no one else existed.

"My son, what has happened? You look distraught."

"I want to hear the truth from your mouth. Am I a foundling? Am I not my parents' true son?"

Seti's hard face sagged and turned pale. A terrible silence. A silence that spoke to the horror in Moses' anguished mind. *Deny it, deny it, deny it!* he prayed in his heart. But his father said nothing, and Moses suddenly knew beyond a shadow of doubt.

"I am the son of slaves!" he moaned, covering his face.

"You are the son the gods preserved and sent to us."

But only one word came through to Moses.

"Preserved!" he said, in awful tones. "Preserved—from what?"

"From a decree—that was needful."

Moses gazed imploringly into the hooded eyes of *the man he called Father.* His voice trembled.

"The painting on the wall. The children . . . Tell me you didn't do it."

Seti turned his head away. After an endless pause, he spoke.

"The Hebrews grew too numerous. They might have risen against us and overwhelmed us through sheer force of numbers. For the greater good, sometimes sacrifices must be made."

For a moment, Moses was speechless. Then he cried out: "Sacrifices? You use the holy name of sacrifice to describe tearing babies from their mothers' arms and feeding them to beasts?"

Seti reached out to embrace him but he shrank back.

"Oh, my son," the Pharaoh said. "They were only slaves."

Moses stared at him with the blank eyes of total shock. The man standing before him was some deceiving monster—not his father. He turned and ran blindly away.

He never remembered how he passed what little remained of the night. When he came to himself it was morning, and he was lying with his head in his mother's lap in her private garden, near the reed-pool carved from the river.

He stared at the water for a long time with dull eyes and let her stroke his hair. At last he said: "Was it here you found me?"

"Yes."

"In the basket."

"Yes."

"Why did you keep it?"

"It brought me a beloved son."

"It makes everything I believed in a lie."

She made him sit up and face her. "But, Moses, it isn't! You are our son, and we love you!"

"Why me? Why was I alone, of all my generation, preserved?"

"The gods willed it."

"And did they will the deaths of the others?"

There was a long pause. The Queen, however she might want to spare him and be loyal, could not blaspheme.

"No. That, your father willed."

"What kind of man does that?"

She stood up and spoke to him sternly.

"Moses, you may not speak against your father. Listen to me. Everything we have here is built on the work of our slaves. Without them, there is no way that our precious traditions could be carried on. No way that your father, your brother, or you—or I— could live and build and die and be buried, and be remembered, as is fitting."

"But Mother—"

"No, Moses, you must understand. We would have to live like humble folk, and, far, far worse, when we die, go down into blowing sand, and rot, and be forgotten.

"Greatness, my dear son, is built upon one thing: power. And power means being strong where others are weak. Command is a word without meaning unless there are those who obey.

"But even slaves, wretched and powerless though they appear, existing only to do our bidding, could endanger everything we hold dear, if they became too many. Your father could not, for the honor of his dynasty, for the sake of the order and prosperity of our nation, allow their numbers to grow without restraint."

Moses stared at her. "But if he murdered a whole generation—who did he think would be his slaves if no new Hebrew children were born?"

His mother looked away. "The males. He culled only the males. The girl-infants he spared."

Moses' mind was churning with horror upon horror. *Culled!* It was too ruthless—too callous—too calculating!

His mother rushed to him and laid her hands on his forehead as if to control his thoughts. "Moses, don't, don't think about it! When the gods give you the gift of a fortunate life, you must repay them by enjoying it. Forget the rest!"

Moses stood, stiff and stark. *My father is a tyrant.*

My brother will follow in his footsteps. Where am I in all this? Am I part of it—part of the guilt and horror? Am I something I can't even think about? Or—am I nothing at all?

But he loved his mother still, and did not say the words aloud.

CHAPTER 7

A Vision
AND A
Death

" oses, I can't wait to tell you! I haven't told anyone yet. Are you listening?"

"Yes."

"You have a funny look in your eye, as if you—
Moses! What are you gazing out over the brickfields
for? There's nothing interesting there! Look at *me*,
will you?"

Rameses shook his brother by the shoulder and
Moses' eyes slowly returned to him. Then Rameses
said solemnly:

"Last night, the gods granted me a vision. I'm not
merely going to restore this temple. I'll make it more
grand, more splendid than any other monument in
Upper or Lower Egypt!"

The two brothers were standing together, observ-
ing the work in progress on the damaged temple.
Several days had passed since Moses found out the
truth of his history. He was struggling to come to
terms with it, and so far he had failed.

His parents had done all they could to make him forget, and his mother had begged him to say nothing to Rameses. "He has so much responsibility now," she said. "Whatever you can say of *us, he* is in no way to blame."

So now Moses listened in silence as Rameses moved his hand dreamily over the scene, and then spread out a papyrus sheet on which was a grandiose design.

"I drew this sketch as soon as I woke. Look! Did you ever see anything so magnificent? Could I have drawn this without the gods' inspiration? Throughout all time to come, men will gaze upon this temple and say, 'It was the great Rameses who built this!' I shall bring everlasting honor to my father and my future children, and to the gods!"

But Moses' mind was elsewhere. He was listening to a sound he had heard all his life but only now heard with his inmost soul—the cracking of a whip.

From nearby came the sound of an overseer's harsh voice.

"Get up, dog! I will *make* you move!"

As Rameses talked excitedly on, about new temples he meant to erect to various gods, Moses stared over his shoulder. Around him toiled numberless slaves. Their ceaseless labors stirred the dust so that a perpetual pall hung over them. He drew in a deep breath, tasted dust, and thought how difficult it must be for them to breathe.

He saw how poorly dressed they were, how their sandals were cracked and dangling, how some had none, and he thought of the heat of the sand at mid-day. He saw how the covering on their bent backs was scarcely enough to keep off the sun. Sometimes they were half-naked, their rags torn off them by the overseer's lash. On skin and rags there were often stripes of dark blood that soaked up the dust.

He saw how their thin arms strained to lift the loads, and imagined the state of their bare hands that had to rub all day against stone made rougher by clinging sand.

He remembered that once as a child he had decided to build a dam in play. He had made mud bricks as he had seen the slaves do, mixing them with bits of straw, and then, impatient, had picked up some large stones and heaped them up. In half an hour his nails were broken and filthy and the skin of his hands blistered; he had run back to the palace, crying to be washed and rubbed with ointments.

He remembered how, years later, his chariot wheels had got stuck in the sand, and he had had to push and shove it himself until his back and arms and legs had ached and he had thought himself a hero for his unaccustomed efforts.

He suddenly saw that these slaves were *men and women*, human beings like him. His mind magnified his little half-forgotten aches, and in his remembering muscles he had an inkling—no more—of the huge carpet of suffering stretched out all around him. And compassion took him in a crushing grip.

As he saw the whip raised to crack down upon a bent back, something landed on his own shoulders and made him start as if he felt the agony of the lash.

"Why are you so nervous? You jumped like a startled cat!" laughed Rameses, who had just thrown his arm around him. "Did you hear what I said? Fate has turned our little misadventure into a great opportunity! Father will be so proud of what we will do together, you and I. Look, look up there! Where that column is being erected. High, you think? That is nothing! That is just the beginning. I will build the highest temples that have ever been seen in Egypt!"

But Moses' eyes were upon an old man on a stone platform in the midst of the half-built temple. He was struggling to raise a piece of dressed stone. It was a load for three men, but the overseer was well aware of the princes watching him and he was determined to show the work he could get out of even this old slave.

"Lift! Lift the stone when I order it!"

He struck the straining back again and again with his whip, but the poor old man quite simply had not the strength to obey.

"And here, there will be a statue of Hapi, god of the Nile, flanked by two great columned halls—" Rameses was saying excitedly.

The whip fell again. Moses jerked as if he felt it in his own flesh. And at that very moment he became aware of Miriam.

He had no reason to look around suddenly and see her. But he did. She was passing close to him, carrying a basket of sand, and she had stopped on her way and was gazing at him. Now he saw her in daylight, even through the miasma of dust, he saw that she was indeed his sister, because the eyes he stared into for that brief moment were the eyes he saw in the polished bronze *ankh* each day.

She looked at him and then up at the old man who was being beaten and it was as if, across the space dividing them, she spoke to him.

Someone must put a stop to it.

Something exploded in Moses' brain. He brushed past Miriam and several other sand-carriers, ran to the foot of the platform and swarmed up the ladder. The cracking of the whip drowned out every other noise.

He seemed to *feel* the sound as pain in his whole body. The ladder seemed endless, but at last he reached the top. The overseer had his back to him. His voice shouting "Lift! Lift! Lift!" was like drumbeats keeping time as his whip-arm rose and fell.

Moses could not bear it. "Stop!" he screamed. "Stop! Stop!"

He ran at the man and jumped on to his back.

"Moses—!"

He heard Rameses' shocked shout. Then the man, caught completely off-balance, fell forward under him. Moses fell too, and the two of them were toppling off the platform together when Moses felt a grip on his ankle. This held him back just long enough to enable him to regain his balance and save himself from following the overseer onto the stone floor below.

What followed was confusion. There were voices raised from all sides—screams and cries, roars of dismay from the overseers, and Rameses' voice shouting, "Moses! Moses! I'm coming!"

Moses looked around and saw the old slave releasing his ankle. For a moment their eyes met; then the man crawled quickly away, slid over the edge of the platform, and was gone.

Next moment the head of a guard appeared at the top of the ladder. Below, Moses could hear others shouting, "What's happened here? Who did this?" and other voices replying, "Up there! He's up there!" The guard came up onto the platform, followed by another, and when they saw Moses their anger turned to bewilderment.

Now Moses could hear the Hebrews talking excitedly below, then the guards cracking their whips and driving them away with shouts of "Get on with your work, there's nothing to gape at, have you never seen a dead man before?"

A dead man . . . He had killed someone!

Moses panicked. He didn't know himself any more, nor understand what motivated him to feel and move and act. He leaped off the platform on the other side, and fled.

As he ran he thought for a moment that he saw Miriam, and that she reached out a hand to him, as if to hold him back. But it was probably an illusion like everything else. In that moment, nothing in the world seemed real.

He was on the outskirts of the city before he heard Rameses' chariot closing on him from behind and heard him call: "Moses! Stop! Moses!"

He didn't stop, but the chariot overtook him, swerved to a halt in front of him, and Rameses leapt off and grabbed him by the shoulders.

Moses tried to free himself. "Let me go!"

"No—wait—"

"You saw what happened. I killed a man."

"Yes, I saw it. You didn't mean to kill him, you just flew into a rage. But why? Why?"

Moses stared at him for a full minute. His brother's face held more concern than anger, but to Moses he seemed a stranger.

"I had to," he said at last. "He was beating my— brother."

"What? Are you mad? He was beating an old slave. I'm your only brother." Rameses shook him.

"No. That's a lie. Everything is a lie. I'm not your brother."

"What are you talking about?"

"Ask the man I once called Father."

He moved out of Rameses' grip and walked away.

"Moses—you have nothing to fear!"

Moses stopped but did not turn around. *Nothing to fear?*

"You won't be punished! I am Pharaoh's heir. I will make it as if it never happened!"

The death of the overseer—yes. Rameses could

wipe that out with a word, a gesture. But he could not wipe out Moses' guilt at the ending of a man's life. He could not wipe away Moses' loss of himself and of his whole family—of *his* life. No earthly power could make that as if it had never happened.

Moses shook his head in a spasm, and began to run.

CHAPTER 8

WANDERINGS

When Moses fled, leaving everything safe, comfortable and familiar far behind, he did not do it by choice. He did it because he couldn't help it. He was like the shell of a man, with his heart torn out, his brain blown hollow like an egg, a man who had lost himself, whose only feeling was despair and the need to escape.

Even to his body's safety he gave no thought. He was half a day's walk out in the desert before the fundamental need for water occurred to him, and that was only because he began to hallucinate. He smelled the water first, and then saw patches of it glistening on the sand ahead. His legs carried him toward the mirage with an eagerness that overruled his head, which told him, "It's not water, but that doesn't matter, because nothing matters."

Nevertheless, the glittering false pools drew him on and on. Looking at them detachedly while his legs stumbled toward them, he saw again the River Nile and the pool in his mother's pleasure garden, and heard her voice telling him lies about his being her son.

When night came, he collapsed. It was then, as the moon rose, that he thought of the Queen as his mother for the last time, remembering that he had not said good-bye to her and that she would grieve and that he would never see her again. He lay on the chilling sand and wept like a child, spilling, in his tears, water that his body could ill afford.

The next day he rose before dawn and stumbled on, going east toward the sunrise. Why east? He tried to think about it. East because that was where the Hebrews were said to have come from, hundreds of years ago. *I am walking home,* he thought. His thoughts were becoming crazed.

The sun came up and climbed the sky and Moses tried to pray to Ra, the sun-god, to protect him, but to no avail. Ra seemed to know he was deserting Egypt and beat upon him without mercy. After some hours, the horsehair wig still on his head seemed like the weight of a block of masonry, and he tore it off and threw it down. The sand blew over it and swallowed it. He paused, swaying, and watched this happen. A strange thought came: *The prince in me is drowned dead in this desert.*

Some time later, he pulled off the heavy gold jewelry from his neck and arms, and dropped them. Then he tore the ring from his finger. But when he looked at it, with its beautiful Nile-green stone, he thought of Rameses who had given it to him. He heard Rameses' voice, full of care for him, shouting, "Moses! Stop! Moses!" Rameses was untainted by the lies. *He* had not betrayed him. He was not his brother; yet in Moses' heart, he still was. Moses slowly replaced the ring, and wandered on. It hung on his hand like a dead weight.

Time slowed to a crawl.

It was another lie that nothing mattered. Thirst mattered. It was all that did. Every other luxury he had abandoned was nothing. Only water counted.

As he stumbled on under the hammer strokes of the midday sun, he remembered his mother saying that if they had no slaves they would die and rot and the sand would cover them. For a royal person, this end was unthinkable. Pharaohs never died as lesser men died; their bodies did not rot, they were preserved by the embalmers' art and would exist forever in magnificent sarcophagi, entombed in eternal splendor.

But Moses knew that if he allowed himself to die here and fall in the sand, he would have his bones picked clean and scattered by wild creatures. He would have nothing, no food or ornament or clothing or treasure for the afterlife. His *ka*—his spirit—if it survived such indignities—would be as beggarly before the gods as any slave's. And he felt the shame of a pharaoh's son, even though he knew he was none.

Rather than die like that, he kept going.

On the third day Ra took pity, as Moses supposed, and covered his burning eye with a cloud. But it was a false hope. The wild pagan gods of the desert had defeated Ra with a cloud that was not of the sky but of the ground. And Moses, in his dried-out exhaustion, raised his eyes and saw that the cloud had conquered the horizon too, and was rushing toward him like a mighty wave.

He threw himself down into a dip and muffled his face with his hands. But he did not hope to live. As the sandstorm roared over him, covering him with its myriad grains that stung like insects, he struggled to say his death-prayers to the gods of Egypt, but he couldn't remember which ones should receive them. As breathing became more difficult, he thought, *The Hebrews have only one god. That must make prayer easier.* Then he lost consciousness.

A sharp pain on top of his head drew him back.

He struggled against the bonds of sand that held him on all sides. He could still draw thin breaths but he could not open his eyes. He felt another sharp tug. Something was pulling his hair!

He felt himself being dragged forth into sunlight. He struggled fiercely and freed his arms. He opened sand-clogged eyes.

A camel with foul breath was bent over him, busily eating his hair.

He shouted at it as best he could, through a mouth lined with sand, and it lazily moved away, chewing a mouthful of hair and gurgling. This was no mirage! Moses scrambled out of the sand dune sculpted by the scouring wind. He had his eyes fastened on a water bag hanging from the empty saddle.

He started to run, fell, got up again, and with the last of his strength, caught up with the camel. He managed to grasp the trailing rope and pulled the brute to a stop. He grabbed the bag, lifted it from its place, unstoppered it, and poured the elixir it contained down his parched throat. Instantly, all else was forgotten in his renewed desire to live.

He was too weak to mount the camel, but he let it tow him where it would. He knew that it must have escaped somehow and that it would take him to water. He also knew that in the desert, where there is water, there are people.

Sure enough, after half an hour he saw a small oasis of palms with a big, square-topped well at its center, around which was the usual watering trough for animals. As he drew nearer, he could see a flock of fat-tailed sheep jostling to get near the trough, which was already occupied by a group of camels. Some men, clearly camel drivers, were standing nearby with their backs to him.

Moses, behind his camel, dipped his head, shoulders, and arms into the god-sent water and drank some more. Then he gave his attention to the little scene being played out near him.

The camel drivers had strong staves with which they were barring the way of the sheep, whose attendants—three little girls in nomadic garb—were pleading with the men to let their sheep drink.

"Oh, please! We drew this water for *our* animals, and your camels are drinking it all!"

"Yes," said a little thing barely high enough to peep over a sheep's back, "we worked hard, we are all in a *sweat*!"

The men roared with laughter.

"Sweat is healthy for girls! Work up a new one, *biti*, it will water you and make you grow!"

"Why do you call me your daughter?" said the child indignantly. "I am *not* your daughter! My father is the High Priest of Midian!"

"'My father is the High Priest of Midian!'" squeaked another of the men, mocking her. "Oh, I am so fearful of the High Priest's anger!"

Moses stood up. The High Priest of *where*, had she said?

The men had now moved away a little, jeering at the children and prodding their sheep with their staves to drive them farther off. The girls were beginning to cry. This would not do. Moses crept around under cover of the well wall and, standing among the men's beasts, suddenly called out, "Aren't these your camels?"

The men spun round, startled. Moses picked up an abandoned stave. "Because I think they're anxious to be moving on," he said calmly.

He gave the nearest camel a blow with the stave. It reared its head out of the trough with a trumpet note of alarm.

The men started back toward the well in fury, but Moses was laying about him, thwacking the camels' rumps and driving them away from the water. They were jostling and rearing and turning, blocking the men's path. *"Hut-hut-hut!"* shouted Moses, and the camels, hearing the order to run, stampeded, scattering their masters before heading into the open desert. The men had no choice but to give chase, though shouting curses and threats back over their shoulders.

The little girls clustered around Moses.

"Where did you come from? Are you the spirit of the well?"

"Silly! He's a man."

"And a good one," said the eldest. "Thank you, stranger."

Moses, quite drained by the effort he had made, backed away from them, for they were crowding him now, touching his garments, still stiff with sand, and peering up at him inquisitively.

"Why have you no beard? Why is your hair so short?" they asked with childish curiosity, reaching up their hands to touch his face. He backed further, fell against the wellhead, which crumbled, letting him topple backwards into the well!

It was a long way down, and the splash as he hit the water echoed eerily. The water was staggeringly cold. He went under, then shot up, spluttering, and trod water, and shouted up at the little faces he could see ringing the well top.

"Get me out! Lower the bucket and pull me up!"

"Yes! We will! Don't drown, bare-face, please don't drown!" came their birdlike voices.

The bucket, a heavy leather one, came down on the end of a rope. Moses felt suddenly afraid. He was too big! They would never pull him up, three little girls, how could they? But it seemed they could. Slowly, painfully, they wound the winch and hauled him cubit by cubit to the top. What strength these desert-bred children had!

But they had not done it alone.

Just as Moses' head was about to clear the well, another face appeared. And this one startled him so much that he almost lost his hold on the bucket. For he recognized it.

It was the Midianite girl!

CHAPTER 9

A DESERT WELCOME

"Y ou!" She gave him one look of disdain and let go the rope.

He jerked down two cubits and thought he must plunge to the bottom again. But her little sisters (for so they proved to be) hung on with all their might so that he dangled just below the well mouth, one hand reaching up to clutch the ledge. He could hear them screaming:

"Tzipporah, don't let go! Help us pull him up!"

"Let him drop. He is not worth saving."

"But he saved *us*!"

She—*Tzipporah*, beautiful name—stared down into his face in the shadow of the well. Her own was in dazzling sunlight and looked to him like Isis, the goddess of magic who could put the shattered dead back together.

"He is a bare-face from the great city of builders!"

"He chased the bad men away!"

"Don't be afraid of him!"

"Afraid?" she said contemptuously, and with a couple of strong pulls on the rope she brought him up again. Giving her no time to change her mind, Moses "walked" up the last of the wall and swung himself to safety through the broken gap.

He stood facing her. She was on home ground here; he was the stranger, and, as he well knew, quite at her mercy. If she chose she could have him driven from the oasis.

"How did he save you?" she asked the girls.

They gathered at her skirts, all talking at once, and she embraced them as she listened, but she was still looking measuringly at him.

At last, she addressed him. "So. We are in your debt, it seems. Did you chase me all this way from Egypt?"

"No, lady."

"But you did find my camel."

"Oh! Is he yours? It was he who found me. And he saved my life."

"With *my* water bag, without which *I* nearly died."

Moses found his sad and weary mouth twitching.

"Did you fall off? You, a daughter of the desert?"

"Even one who has ridden camels from childhood may be *thrown* off once in a while."

"What a foolish camel, to throw away such treasure," murmured Moses.

"You are the fool. Don't spill your silly words on me, or I may forget the laws of hospitality. Come."

She turned on her heel and led the way back to the Midianite camp, leaving the three little ones to bring Moses after, clinging to his hands and smiling up at him encouragingly.

"Do not mind her," whispered one. "Father says she will never marry because she is so hard on men."

"Why is she?"

"She says they are rough and rude and too hairy."

"Ah! Then she may like a smooth, polite bareface like me," said Moses, and they burst out into giggles. The smallest one giggled so hard she sat down in the sand and couldn't get up. Moses picked her up and carried her the rest of the way on his back. Her little body felt tough and strong, and her hands round his neck were hard as a monkey's paws. Could the daughter of a high priest of Egypt have such hands?

When they got to the camp, which was made up of a number of black goat-hair tents, Tzipporah made him wash behind a screen and gave him clean clothes. He put on the long robe of a desert nomad. He felt naked without his wig, but when he had swathed his head in a cloth in the local fashion, he felt almost comfortable. He emerged shyly, and she inspected him.

"Yes, you will do. Now you're fit to meet my father. But remember. He is our High Priest, and thus as important in our world as your father the Pharaoh is in yours."

"The Pharaoh is not my father," said Moses quietly.

"Indeed! So you are not a prince of Egypt?"

"I was called so, but the truth is otherwise."

She looked at him with more interest than before.

"It was as a prince that I was offered to you at the banquet. What would you have done, if I had not escaped?"

He looked at the ground. "I think I would have wooed you a little."

"Truly," she said after a moment, "you are not the man I took you for."

At that moment the tent-flap burst open and a large, burly man strode in, sending before him a sort of shock wave of energy. He had a full black beard and a booming voice that seemed to bounce off the black tent walls.

"Ah! My honored guest! You are most welcome!" He seized Moses in a bone-crushing hug, lifting him off his feet. "You have been sent as a blessing! Tonight we will entertain you. You will not be a stranger in our land!"

He dropped Moses back on his feet and swept out again as abruptly as he had come.

"Your father, I presume?" said Moses, somewhat breathless.

She nodded, smiling. "Jethro. He will make a big fuss of you. Do not let it go to your head."

"A big fuss"—to whit, a feast—among the Midianites was in its way as lavish as one in Pharaoh's palace, and a great deal more enjoyable, Moses thought.

The tribesmen gathered in another, much larger tent, festooned with bright hangings, and floored with coarse but colorful rugs, embroidered cushions, and rank-smelling sheepskins. The women were not to be seen, but pleasanter smells from outside told what they were busy with. Girl-children, however, were allowed, and Tzipporah's little sisters crept up to him in their best clothes—small black gowns beautifully embroidered—and showed him where to seat himself and how to behave.

When a huge communal dish of yellow rice piled with spicy meat was laid before Moses, his hungry hand reached out at once, but the middle sister tugged his sleeve. "Not yet!" she whispered urgently. "You must wait for Father."

"Oh!" said Moses, ashamed. In Egypt, no one might eat until *he* was present and gave the signal.

Jethro entered in a rush as before, accompanied by several young men—his sons, no doubt. He bowed smilingly before Moses and sat in the place of honor beside him. Silence fell upon the chattering guests.

"My children, let us give thanks for the bounty of nature and for the excellence of trade! And also for the coming of this brave young man whom we honor here tonight."

Moses flushed. "I have done nothing in my life worth honoring."

Jethro jerked back his head in comic astonishment, and fairly roared: "Wha-a-at's that you say? First you rescue Tzipporah from captivity in your country, then you defend my younger daughters from brigands! Is that nothing?"

"Rescue Tzipporah from—?"

"She has told me *all*. Now, my son, not another word! First we will eat, for you must be half-starved. Then we will have music, in which I delight, and we will see if Egyptians can dance."

Moses glanced at the girls. They raised their brows, grinned and nodded toward the food, which had multiplied, as veiled women slipped in and out of the tent bringing the dishes of crushed chickpeas puddled with olive oil, goat's cheese beaten to a cream and scattered with olives, mounds of steaming burghal, fragrant with sage and hyssop and dotted with raisins, and bowls of curd. Baskets of flat, hot bread pouches with which to scoop up the food were passed around. To follow was sweet sticky rice, perfumed with rose water and honey and spiked with nuts, and a mountain of pomegranates, figs, and dates.

Moses had thought he would never enjoy anything again; he had given up the very notion of pleasure. He had courted death. Yet life does not let go so easily, and when the heart is young it is very hard to break. He surprised himself by eating, and drinking, with great enthusiasm.

While they feasted, Jethro spoke to him.

"My boy, Tzipporah has told me how you lived in Egypt. You'll find quite a change if you stay with us! Not that I'm apologizing for our modest way of life. We have what is more precious to us than riches and palaces—freedom. Freedom to move about, given us by our tents. Freedom to do our own work, which is to say, freedom from the shame of living by the work of others. Eat! Eat! Have you lost the use of your hands?"

Moses said, "Freedom is valuable only to those who know where they belong, and—and who they are."

"H'm," said the old man, his mouth full of roast goat. "Of course I know nothing of your circumstances, but my years have taught me one thing. It's not given to us to see the full design, still less what our part is in the pattern."

Moses was puzzled.

"We are all part of a grand design, like little colored threads in a vast carpet," said Jethro, clapping him on the back. "No thread is more or less important than the next."

He tapped Moses' green-stoned ring with one rough finger. "Our worth is not determined by what we have, but by what we do with it. If you look at your life this way, through heaven's eyes, you will understand your value. Trust this, and your confusion will leave you."

When the musicians appeared in the tent mouth, with their strange instruments and desert drums, and began to invite the company with a wild, provoking tune, the wine he had drunk seemed to lift Moses to his feet as soon as the eldest of the three girls tugged his hand.

She led him outside where a big fire burned, throwing sparks up amid the stars, and before he knew it he was whirling around in a circle, dancing to the beat of the drums and the shrill half-tones of pipes and strings, lost and yet wondrously found again.

And in the firelit darkness he saw, among the women, modest in the shadows, Tzipporah's face come and go and come again as the circle whirled him past her—that beautiful, proud, angry face that was not angry now, but mysteriously, tenderly smiling.

painting by Paul Lasaine

In ancient Egypt, the slaves toil to erect great tributes to Pharaoh.

To escape the guards who seek to fulfill Pharaoh's decree that all newborn Hebrew males be killed, Yocheved, Miriam, and Aaron hurry to the banks of the Nile River.

The basket—with the infant Moses inside—floats toward the palace.

Moses witnesses the brutal beating of a slave.

Feeling lost and alone, Moses sets out across the blazing desert sand.

Moses makes his way to Midian and starts a new life as a shepherd.

One day, while tending his sheep, Moses comes upon a burning bush.

To demonstrate God's power, Moses uses his staff to turn the Nile River to blood.

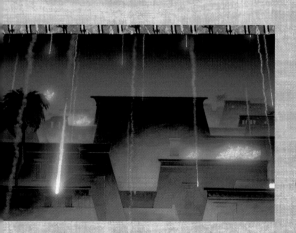

When Pharaoh refuses to listen to God's command, a barrage of plagues—including hailfire—rain down on Egypt.

The Angel of Death silently drifts through the streets of Egypt.

painting by Paul Lasaine and Ron Lukas

Moses leads the Hebrew people on their exodus out of Egypt.

Once again drawing on God's power, Moses parts the waters of the Red Sea.

The Hebrews look back triumphantly toward Egypt.

painting by Paul Lasaine

Months later, Moses presents his people with God's Ten Commandments.

PART TWO

CHAPTER 10

THE BURNING BUSH

O f all times of day, Moses loved the dawn best. In the old days, in Egypt, he had seldom seen the dawn—princes don't tend to rise early. And the sky behind the great city was always obscured by smoke, and dust, and buildings. But here in the desert, dawn was a recurring blessing, and every morning for the fifteen years since he had come here, Moses had witnessed it without ever tiring of its beauty.

Today he rose as usual in darkness made darker by the impenetrable black walls of the tent he shared with his wife. He kissed her blindly as she lay in their bed of sheepskins. She would get up soon, to make food for him and to attend to their two young sons, Gershom and Eliezer. Meanwhile he touched her hair and whispered tenderly, "I love you, little bird." That was the meaning of her name.

He slipped outside to wash in the water she had

prepared for him. He splashed it—desert-night-cold—all over his body, and dipped his whole head in the leather bucket. He rubbed his hands over it. He was not a "bare-face" any longer, but wore the free-growing hair and beard of his adopted people.

When he raised his dripping face, and looked east, he could see the first thin streaks of gold against the darkness. Here came the sun disk of Great Ra, reborn, as it was each day, of Nut, the sky goddess! The sun's first rays shot over the horizon, which was as cleanly drawn as a knife-cut in the clear desert air.

He strode back into the tent. Tzipporah was awake and had kindled the fire and heated milk flavored with cardamom and honey for him.

"Where will you take the sheep today?" She was whispering, to let the boys sleep a little longer.

"Oh, I don't know," he said, slipping on his robe. "Grazing is poor everywhere. I'll see where they lead me."

"Here, take your food." She handed him a hide pouch of bread and goat's cheese, some dried figs, and his water bottle. Then she poured the milk from the *finjan* into a clay cup for him. He stood in the tent mouth, sipping, watching the dawn turn into day, aware of loving the great clean sparkling desert, and his simple life as a shepherd and a family man.

Aware of missing nothing he had left, except sometimes Rameses.

But there was a dark something under all the satisfaction, a feeling of unease—of something left undone—that never quite left him, even at his happiest. He tried not to think about it or allow it to poison his life.

Today he was peaceful in himself; the nagging ache was quiet. He little knew what this ordinary day now breaking would bring him.

Staff in hand, he strode along behind his father-in-law's flock.

It was high summer. The little green that had sprung up after the sparse rainfall of spring had become dry and most of it had been grazed off by the flocks for miles around the nomad camp, which had already been moved three times.

Every day he had to walk farther, and even so, the fat-sacks under the sheeps' tails were flaccid, and their udders yielded less and less milk. Watching the sheep snatching at tussocks already cropped to the roots, Moses thought, *It's time to move again.*

He and the sheep walked, and paused, and walked, with Moses keeping a careful watch on landmarks invisible to anyone but a desert wanderer, so he could find his way home at day's end. Every now and then he counted heads. At noon he ate in the scant shade of a scrawny acacia tree, then dozed. When he woke he counted again, and found one sheep missing.

He scouted about for tracks, and found them, leading off toward a narrow canyon in an outcropping of red rocks. The flock was busy with some salt bushes, so Moses, grumbling to himself, set off in quest of the lost sheep.

It was wiser than he. It had found both shade and fodder in the mouth of the canyon, and it didn't want to leave. When Moses tried to drive it back to the others, it dodged him and ran deeper into the canyon, around some rocks.

Moses followed.

His eyes found the dark shadow of the rocks difficult to penetrate, after the brilliant sunshine outside them, and he was walking with his staff outstretched. When he turned the corner, he stopped suddenly, and his mouth fell open.

In his path was a bright light. It half-blinded him.

He shielded his eyes, then looked again. An incredible sight! A dry bush that, lit with tinder, would have blazed to ashes in a minute. But this one burned, and burned, and was not consumed.

Moses could see the leaves and twigs within the ball of flame, unaffected by the heat. And the fire was no ordinary fire. It dazzled and shone like a giant crystal with torchlight behind it and all around it.

Moses was suddenly deeply afraid.

Fear shot up in him like a flame itself, and when it was at its height, a voice spoke to him from out of the burning bush.

"Moses. Moses. Moses. Moses."

Moses stood perfectly still. The flame of fear within him shrank but did not go out. The flame in the bush before him burned on as before.

Again, the voice called him, and this time he answered through bone-dry lips, "Here I am."

"Take the shoes from off thy feet, for the place on which thou standst is holy."

Was it a true voice, or was it inside his head? It had a timbre, a resonance that was not of this world. Moses stooped and unlatched his sandals and stepped out of them onto the rock.

"Who are you?" he found courage to ask.

"I am—that I am."

"I don't understand," said Moses humbly.

"I am the God of thine ancestors, Abraham, Isaac, and Jacob."

These names meant nothing to Moses. But their solemnity made his knees buckle. He planted his staff between his bare feet and kept upright.

"What do you want with me?" he whispered.

"I have seen the oppression of my people in Egypt and I have heard their cry. I have come to deliver them out of slavery and bring them to the land I promised to their forebears, a land flowing with milk and honey. And so unto Pharaoh I shall send thee."

The words held such irresistable command that Moses felt he might lose consciousness with the terror of them. But he roused himself to cry out: "No, Lord, not I! I cannot. I will not find words."

"I shall teach thee what to say."

"He will not believe me. He will not listen."

"Who made man's mouth? Who made the deaf, the mute, the seeing, and the blind? Will I not open men's ears to my words that I will give thee? Now go!"

The fire from the bush seemed to leap toward him as if to drive him away. He backed, terror-stricken, against the canyon wall.

"You who are—that you are—have pity! I am not your messenger! Your people hate me, for I was the son of the man who murdered their children! How can I move them with my stumbling tongue?"

"Oh Moses, I shall be with thee! Thou shalt go

before Pharaoh and say unto him, Let my people go."

Moses shook his head in a spasm.

"No, Lord. I cannot."

And now the voice rose to a roar like wind-driven fire.

"I say thou shalt! And I know that the king of Egypt will not give you leave to go, except by a mighty hand. And I will put forth my hand and smite Egypt with all my wonders. And after that he will let you go."

So mighty and terrible were these words that Moses dared not speak, but God could read his thoughts.

"Art thou still afraid? Take thy staff in thy hand and do wonders with it! Thou art what I would have thee be, and thy name shall be blessed throughout the generations of my people Israel. I am with thee, Moses."

The blinding light from the bush seemed to flow toward him, but there was no heat, no terror now. It wrapped him in itself and he felt unearthly peace, strength, and resolve flowing through him. He bowed himself to the ground. When he dared raise his face, the fire had gone, and the bush was—just a bush. His lost sheep was nibbling at its leaves. Of the voice, nothing remained; only the soft whistling of the wind through the canyon broke the silence.

He looked about him, dazed. Then he put on his

sandals, picked up his staff, and gently touched the sheep with it. It seemed to start, and then, responding to Moses' chirruping call, trotted obediently ahead of him back to the others.

Just before rounding a bend that would remove the bush from his sight, Moses turned for one last look at it. He was not even surprised to see that it was covered with blossoms.

CHAPTER 11

MOSES
THE
MESSENGER

"**B**ut Moses! What can one man do against the mighty Pharaoh?"

"One man alone can do nothing. One man and God can do anything."

He had told Tzipporah what had happened. It was hard for her to believe, but so was the change in Moses. From being a mere man (though one she deeply loved) he had become as one driven by an energy and a determination she had never seen in him, or any man, before.

"It's dangerous. Why should Pharaoh free his slaves? Do you understand what that would mean for him?"

"Far better than you! But he must and will do it. The suffering of the Hebrew slaves must end. It was not until I lived with your people, who are free, who do their own work with dignity, and decide their own destiny, that I understood how monstrous that suffering is."

Tzipporah brooded, her chin on her hand. "My people have always been free. The Hebrews have been slaves for hundreds of years. What do they know of freedom? If you get them away—and I see you mean to achieve it—you'll have to teach them how to be free men."

Moses stood up decisively. "What are you saying? Freedom is the natural state, they won't need teaching! I must go—now—today! Are you coming with me?"

She rose at his side. "Of course I am. I'll leave the boys with my sisters."

"They will be safe and loved, and in good time your father will bring them to us! Come, my brave one, let's get ready to leave!" he cried, full of vigor and eagerness to set about his great task.

Their journey took three days. Then the first temple appeared on the skyline, then another, and finally the rooftops of the palace. Soon they were riding through the outlying quarries and brickfields, where the slaves were toiling just as they had so long ago.

Riding past them on camelback, Moses was stricken with anguish. For fifteen years he had lived in peace and happiness, while these poor wretched people had been suffering and struggling, living their short, blighted lives, and passing away without hope or dignity. How could he have forgotten them!

Tzipporah, mounted behind him with her arms around his waist, gazed from side to side in horror and amazement.

"I see why you had to come" was all she said.

Moses said nothing, but his thoughts reproved him: *I was made to come. Without God's order I would not have come.*

They rode through the familiar streets to the entrance to the royal palace. The guards crossed their spears before him.

"What do you want, tribesman?" they asked contemptuously.

"I have business with the Pharaoh," said Moses.

They roared with laughter.

"What business is that? Have you lost your goats?"

Moses ignored their mockery. "Tell Seti I am here."

The laughter stopped and the men looked at each other incredulously.

"Truly, these nomads must live with their heads buried in sand! Don't you know the old Pharaoh traveled to the next world three years ago?"

Moses gasped. "So the new Pharaoh is—"

"Rameses the Second, of course!"

Ah! Rameses! This might not be so hard.

"Take me to him!" Moses shouted joyfully.

"If we do, he will take our hides. Don't you know, you ignorant *bedu,* that it's the Festival of Ra? He must sacrifice at the temple, and he has many guests."

"Tell him his brother Moses has come."

Now it was the guards' turn to gape. "*Moses!* He's dead."

"No. I am he."

The guards formed up with others and escorted Moses and Tzipporah through the familiar corridors of the palace into the banqueting hall. When they arrived, the guards fell on their faces in deference to the Pharaoh.

Rameses was enthroned on a raised dais, conferring with a number of richly dressed foreign ambassadors, and some of his own officials. The two high priests, Hotep and Huy, much aged, were among the rest. The room was full of people celebrating the festival; many servants moved among them with platters of food and jugs of wine. Musicians were playing.

But Moses had eyes only for Rameses.

The life of a ruler evidently suited him. His clothes were gorgeous. His headdress was a great striped helmet of gold and green with a solid gold snake-and-vulture ornament—symbol of the Pharaoh's godhead and power of life and death—standing out from the front of it. Around his neck he wore a flat jeweled neckpiece, covering half his chest, intricately made of cornelian, lapis, and turquoise set in gold. On his chin was a false, ceremonial beard, braided and gilded with gold dust.

One of the guards crawled all the way to him and whispered his message. Rameses gave a shout and leapt to his feet, scanning the crowd. He spotted Moses immediately in his long black desert robes.

In one bound he had left the dais and ran, straight as an arrow into Moses' arms. Moses could feel him trembling with excitement. Then they looked into each other's eyes.

"Moses! Moses! Can the gods be so good? Brother, is it really you?"

"Yes, Rameses, I've come back."

"And this—? Oh!" Rameses stared at Tzipporah. "Is it? Do my eyes deceive me?"

"This is my wife, Tzipporah of Midian."

Rameses threw his head back with a great laugh.

"This is wonderful! Wonderful! Ra has bestowed the ultimate blessing on me, to celebrate his festival! Come, Moses, come!"

He clutched their arms and hurried them through the wondering crowds to the dais.

"Be silent and listen, my friends! This—quaintly dressed fellow is none other than my long-lost brother, Prince Moses! Is this not a day to celebrate?

Hotep—Huy—prepare for an extra sacrifice in the Temple of Ra."

The old priests stepped forward.

"Majesty—"

"What is it?"

"We are compelled to remind you that this man committed a serious crime."

"For which the penalty is—we are loathe to say it—"

"Death."

There was a shocked silence over all the company. Rameses looked from one priest to the other. Then he said, in a voice that echoed around the vast room, "We are Pharaoh, the Living God. And we say that we pardon *forever* all crimes of which he stands accused, and will have it known that he is our brother, Moses, Prince of Egypt."

Moses stood as one paralyzed. He had not expected this.

"Rameses—"

Rameses slowly took his glaring eyes away from the trembling priests and turned them softly on Moses.

"Yes, my dear brother."

"In my heart, you are indeed my brother. But things cannot be as they were."

"They shall be as I say they are."

"No. The one true God has spoken to me. Now all things are changed, and must change more."

Rameses continued to stare at him, but his eyes now held a warning.

"What do you mean?"

"God commands that you let my people go."

"Your people?"

"The Hebrew slaves are my people."

"Let them go?"

"Free them."

"Your god commanded this, did he?"

"Yes," said Moses firmly.

"And you expect to be believed, that a god spoke to you. No god has ever spoken to me, and I am Pharaoh."

"Rameses, I beg you to believe me. I fear very bad things may happen if you don't."

Rameses looked at him for a few more moments, and then laughed, a harsh, tight laugh. "I hope I am as pious as the next man," he said. "But I will need some proof of this—god you speak of, who gives out such *wholly impossible* commands."

Moses did not know what to do next, but he felt his staff grow warm in his hand and remembered God's words. Grasping it, not knowing what might happen, but full of trust, he threw it on the ground.

For a split second it lay there. Then it stirred, writhed. Its wood turned to sinuous coiling scales. Moses stared at it in a kind of ecstacy. God *was* with him! The staff had became a serpent!

The people on the dais leapt as it struck out at them. Only Rameses did not move.

"Very impressive," he said, in a voice that implied the opposite. "What a *great* worker of wonders this god of yours must be! Hotep! Huy! Give this snake charmer our answer."

What followed was a display of magic such as Moses had witnessed many times in his youth. But he had to admit that the priests' skills had been sharpened over time.

The great room became dark as torches were extinguished. The musicians began to play dramatic music to give atmosphere. The crowd fell back against the walls, leaving the center of the room open. And the priests began to chant the names of many gods.

"Khnum—Pthah—Nephthys—Anubis—"

"Seshmu—Hemsut—Sokar—Mut—"

As each god was named, his or her face appeared through the smoky gloom. The mouths of the great heads appeared to move, proclaiming their fields of authority and their supremacy over all other gods.

Moses could clearly hear Hotep's and Huy's inflections in the distorted voices, and was not overly impressed by the illusion. But the people were. They gasped and exclaimed and even cowered during the more alarming manifestations.

It was a good display, Moses acknowledged. But when the priests produced two snakes of their own, looping and coiling in silhouette against the wall, Moses saw his staff-snake open its jaws and devour them. But the crowd didn't notice. Nor did Rameses. They were preoccupied with the more sensational display, and roared their approval when the torches were rekindled.

"I think that proves my point," said Rameses, who was looking relaxed and triumphant. "Will my guests please amuse themselves for a short time while I speak privately to my brother?" And he strode off the dais and through a side door, beckoning Moses to follow him.

Moses bent, and, without fear, picked up the serpent by the tail. It instantly became a wooden staff again. Did he imagine it, or was it somewhat— thicker than before? When staffs eat snakes, they grow fat. He smiled and wondered if God saw the joke.

CHAPTER 12

MOSES
REVILED

Moses followed Rameses to the apartment that had once been Seti's. He noticed that the guards along the corridors and at the entrance to the private chambers prostrated themselves as Rameses passed. This was a change from the old days, when it was merely the rule that no one might meet the Pharaoh's eyes.

Rameses led the way straight onto a vast balcony that ran the length of the main room. It commanded a magnificent view of the city, already baking in the midday heat. The vista was much changed from Moses' time. More huge houses had been erected for rich men, and there were new public buildings as well. Rameses pointed to a vast structure that was rising to the south, over which slaves were swarming like termites.

"What do you think of that?"

"What is it to be?"

"A temple to Maat, goddess of truth and harmony. When I die, the gods will weigh my heart against the feather in her hair to see if I am fit to join them. I've built four new temples, all adorned with gigantic statues of myself, and work has begun on my own tomb. It is to be dug deep into the solid rock of a mountain. My architects have been ordered to design the inside so that no grave-robbers will ever find the sacred sepulchre and disturb my remains."

"My congratulations," said Moses.

"You approve?"

"You've fulfilled your ambitions."

Rameses laughed. "Not yet! I shall go on building until I die."

"And how many have died already, to give you the immortal fame you crave?"

Rameses stared at him. "No one has died, that I know of."

"Rameses, look out there. What do you see?"

"A greater Egypt than my father saw!"

"That's not what I see."

"Moses, I can't change what *you* see. I have to maintain the ancient traditions. I bear the weight of my father's crown."

"Do you still not understand what Seti was?"

"A very great leader."

"His hands bore the blood of thousands of children."

Moses saw incredulity, and then a bewildered anger, come over his brother's face. "Slaves, do you mean? Moses, be sane! The blood of slaves is of less account than the waters of the Nile, that nourish our fields!"

"Those slaves are my people. The least of them is as dear to God as you."

"Which god are you talking about?"

"Mine. The Hebrew God. The one who spoke to me and ordered me to come back here and say to you, *Let my people go.*"

"So you have come back, not because this is your home or I am your brother. Only to free the slaves."

The two men stared at each other. Moses drew off the heavy emerald ring that had stayed on his finger all through the years, and laid it on the arm of Rameses' throne.

"I'm sorry," he said.

Rameses picked the ring up and turned it in his hand. Moses waited. At last, Rameses looked up and his eyes were as hard as as the gem he held. He said, "I do not know this god. Neither will I let your people go."

He turned to leave the chamber. Moses seized

him by the arm. "Rameses—brother—don't harden your heart! I beg you!"

Rameses freed his arm, and drew himself tall. "I have a son, Moses. And I have told him, as my father told me: Beware the weak link! You may tell 'your people' that from today, their workload has been doubled. They will know who to thank for it."

Moses and Tzipporah left the palace by a rear door.

"How did it go?"

"Very badly. He is going to double the Hebrews' workload."

"How? They work as hard as they can already."

They took their camel and went back to the brickfields. The order that Moses had been told to deliver had reached the overseers already, direct from the Pharaoh, and was causing consternation. Even the foremen of the work brigades didn't know how to put the new order into effect. How could the workload be doubled?

Then an overseer had an idea.

"Instead of bringing straw, ready cut, to the brick makers to be mixed with the mud, we will order the brick slaves to fetch it from the fields. That will free the straw cutters to work making bricks, and if we can force the pace, we may get twice the work out of them."

Moses saw at once this was an idea born of desperation. It would never work, and would simply result in useless labor. But it would make life far harder for all the slaves. They, overhearing and passing the word, knew it too, and began to look about for the cause of their new distress.

"Look! See that man over there? He's in disguise, but I remember him—it's Moses!"

"That's no disguise. He ran away into the desert. He's got no power now, he's just a *bedu*."

"How do you know he hasn't still got the Pharaoh's ear? It must be something he's said to Rameses that's brought on this new order!"

There were rumblings and mutterings. The slaves nearest to him were eyeing him menacingly, and as soon as the foreman went out of sight, one of them picked up a double handful of mud and threw it at him. Moses, startled and hurt, still realized the desperation that lay behind such a dangerous act.

"Go back to the desert," jeered the mud-thrower. "We don't want you here."

"Friend, I've come back to help you."

"Thank you! Your help will kill us with overwork!"

Tzipporah, trying to get the mud off Moses' face and robe, turned on the slave.

"He is only doing what God told him!"

"Which god? Ra? Osiris? Anubis?" sneered another man. "They all despise us and give the Egyptians leave to oppress us!"

"The one true God. Yours. And now mine," said Moses.

A man pushed through the angry crowd that was gathering close to Moses. Moses knew him at once—it was his birth-brother, Aaron—and tried to embrace him. Aaron pushed him away in disgust.

"God?" he almost spat. "When did God start caring about us?"

"He does care! He's seen your suffering and He intends to take you—all of you—out of Egypt and to the Promised Land."

There was a sudden silence, and then Aaron laughed. "Through you, I suppose—his chosen messenger."

"Yes!—Oh, yes!"

The crowd turned. Moses drew in his breath. There stood his sister Miriam, her hands clenched at her sides, her head thrown back. Her hair was graying now, and her lined face showed the hardness of her life, but all that was transfigured.

"Aaron, you shame yourself," she said. Aaron shrank back. So did the others. Miriam walked to

Moses. She gazed up into his face. Her eyes were ablaze so that he could scarcely look at her.

"Moses, hear what I say. I have been a slave all my life, and God has never answered my prayers—until now. God saved you from Seti. He saved you from the river. He saved you in all your wanderings, and even now He saves you from the wrath of Pharaoh. He won't abandon you! And do not *you* abandon us, no matter how the faithless and foolish among us abuse you. Our God has heard our cry at last!" She clasped her hands and turned her face to the sky. "Oh, I can bear anything now!"

The slave crowd was perfectly silent, awed by Miriam's passion. Moses, for his part, felt as if her faith and strength of will flowed into him as she spoke.

But Aaron was not so easily affected. He knew Miriam of old; her diatribes did not move him.

"If God truly sent you," he said cynically, "prove it. Look!" He pointed over Moses' shoulder. "Here comes Pharaoh's barge along the river. Ask him now, if you dare, to free us, and if he refuses—"

"Which he will—" put in several voices.

"—do something to show God's power acting through you! Then we might believe you."

There was a rumble of agreement from the slaves.

Moses looked around at their dirty, work-worn, hopeless faces. He felt the deepest shame of his life for having abandoned them for so long.

"Don't despair," he said pleadingly.

"Despair!" said Aaron. "How dare you breathe the word? Despair is where we live."

Moses felt as if his heart would break.

He turned and walked to the river shore.

THE RIVER
OF
BLOOD

oses stood by the Nile. Tzipporah, Aaron, and the crowd of slaves watched, too, from a safe distance.

As the great barge glided toward him, Moses noticed that on its deck were Hotep and Huy, the priests, entertaining a small boy with some simple tricks. Could this be Rameses' son?

It was. At that moment, Rameses emerged from the bridge and the boy ran to him. He was a sturdy, handsome child with his father's large eyes and strong body. His head was shaved but for the royal sidelock.

The barge drew level with Moses, and he called very loudly: "Rameses!"

Rameses heard him, put the child aside, and came to the rail. "Ho, Moses! And are your people grateful for your intervention on their behalf?"

"Don't mock their misery! Let them go!"

The barge was passing. Rameses called back, "Still gnawing on the same bone?"

"Let—my—people—go!"

"Stop rowing!"

The Pharaoh's order was taken up by other voices into the depths of the ship, and the unseen galley-slaves lifted dripping oars out of the river. The barge slowed, then stopped, and Moses walked along the bank and caught up with it.

"Moses!" shouted Rameses, leaning over the rail. "I have already had enough of your senseless pleas. Be a good fellow and take your wife back to her tribe."

"You ignore me at your peril."

Rameses looked sternly at him across the row of oars. "So it's come to this. You dare threaten the Morning and Evening Star." He straightened. "Guards! Arrest that man."

Five guards instantly jumped over the side and started swimming and wading toward him. Moses stood his ground, though he was full of fear. Then he heard a voice that seemed to blow off the water, the same voice he had heard in the canyon.

"Moses, take thy staff in thy hand and strike the river."

As the men splashed nearer, Moses raised his staff and struck the water of the Nile.

A sinister red stain spread rapidly from the spot. When it reached the guards, they stopped dead, looking down at the water around their knees. One of them bent, dipped his hand in it, and carried it to his nose.

"Blood!" he muttered unbelievingly. And then, in a sudden scream: "The water is blood!"

The guards fled, some back to the ship to be hauled aboard, others to the land. Rameses turned to his priests.

"Explain this!"

They stood, bemused, and then conferred in whispers. Hotep stepped forward. "I think we can demonstrate the superiority of our gods' magic," he said.

He produced a basin of water, made some passes over it with his hand, and the water changed color.

A child's trick, thought Moses. *Rameses cannot be deceived by this!*

But the little boy was jumping up and down, crying "Our gods are better! Our gods are better!" Rameses looked at the red water in the basin, and then at the river—the great River Nile which had turned to blood—and Moses seemed to see the eye of his mind closing.

"Abandon this futile mission, Moses," he called. "Leave Egypt before I wholly lose patience. Remember I am all-powerful and my gods are great." And he gave the signal for the barge to move on.

Moses watched the line of oars swirl in the bloody stream that had been the Nile. Was such a wonder to be compared to a little powder from a priest's sleeve, dropped stealthily into a basin? Was Rameses blind? *Yes.* He was blind as Moses had once been blind to the plight of the slaves—blind because he did not want to see.

Something touched his hand. It was Tzipporah. She had seen the miracle and was pale as death. "What's happening?"

"God said he would show Egypt his wonders. This is just the first."

"But the river—without the waters of the Nile, Egypt will die!"

"God will not let Egypt die of thirst. He has other plans."

He stared after the barge and clutched Tzipporah's hand. It was as if he could see a great destroying storm on the horizon.

At that moment, he heard movement behind him, and turned. It was Aaron, with the crowd of slaves.

"You failed," Aaron said. But he was not jeering.

"Yes," said Moses sadly. "This time."

"Is the river really blood?"

"Yes."

"How will we survive?"

"We must trust in God's mercy."

Aaron looked deep into Moses' eyes. Then, with a simple gesture, he held out his hands. They were lacerated, bruised, raw.

Moses gently took his brother's hands in his and stared into them, trying to comprehend the pain that lay in them—trying, in vain, to share it.

At last he said humbly, "We can't understand the will of God. As my suffering is, compared to yours, we are to Him—grains of sand to his immensity. Perhaps our people needed these centuries of oppression. Perhaps we had to learn the lessons of slavery, so that we shall never offend God by enslaving others. I don't know and I don't pretend to know. I understand only one thing: I am commanded to gain your freedom and lead you to the Promised Land. And I will do it. Please, Brother. Strengthen me with your belief. In God, not in me."

Aaron, moved at last by Moses' tenderness and humility, closed his ruined hands around his brother's in a spasm.

"I will try," he said. "But remember. It's in our flesh that we have felt the centuries. Your flesh has felt nothing."

"That is true," said Moses, in anguish. "That's what makes it all so mysterious. Why me? Why me?" He put back his head and asked of the heavens, "Why me, Lord?"

No answer came. But when he picked up his staff again, he felt it tremble in his hands like a reproach.

CHAPTER 14

THE TIME
OF THE
PLAGUES

A time followed when even Moses' faith was sorely tested.

Not his belief in God. There could be no room for doubt on that score. God proved His existence and His power in the terrible days and weeks that came after Rameses' first refusal. The faith that Moses nearly lost was in God's mercy.

For the punishments were terrible. And nothing Moses could do could make them easier. It was as if God were determined to show the full power of His wrath for all the sufferings heaped on the slaves by the Egyptians, and nothing would stop it.

Time after time Moses came to Rameses. The first time, he said: "Don't you see, this will go on and on, getting steadily worse, until you give in?"

The Pharaoh's face was set in lines of unbreakable stubbornness.

"A few frogs—"

"A few frogs! Rameses, they're everywhere! Even the bread troughs swarm with them, one can't walk without treading on them!"

"It's some natural phenomenon."

And when the people crowded to the palace gates and demanded that the Pharaoh do something, he called Moses and said, "The people insist that I see you. Poor superstitious fools . . . What is it you want, exactly?"

"You know what I want. Let the Hebrews go into the desert to worship their God."

"Just that? Do you think me stupid? They won't come back."

Moses was silent. Then he said, "You want the plague of frogs to end? Let them go."

And Rameses shrugged, nodded, and waved him away. But as soon as the frogs ceased to swarm, he ordered his overseers to work the slaves harder than ever, and to guard them more carefully.

Another plague followed. The people, and their beasts, became covered with lice. Everyone was scratching and tearing at their own flesh; the cattle were half-mad from the bites. Rameses sent for Moses.

"I suppose you're going to say this is your god's doing," he said angrily.

"Has the building work been affected?" asked Moses, knowing the answer.

"No. Lice thrive on *clean* skin. The slaves work on as before, except that the overseers are so busy scratching they can't whip them."

"Doesn't that tell you anything? There were no frogs in the Hebrews' bread troughs, either."

Rameses stared at him. "You're lying," he snarled. "But what does it matter? My ministers demand that I free the slaves. Who do they imagine will build when they have gone? Idiots! But go. Go on, may Osiris take the lot of you—go!"

Moses left the palace elated. But even before he could tell Aaron and the others the good news, the lice had vanished and the order to free the slaves had been rescinded.

The next day clouds of flies began alighting on every edible thing, and that included not only food but living flesh. They crawled and ate and stung and swarmed, and again the people, unable to eat the food that was hidden under coats of flies, maddened by stings, brought petitions before Pharaoh. His advisers, likewise tormented, urged him to release the slaves.

This time Moses didn't allow himself to get excited when Pharaoh told him to take his people and leave. He knew it would not happen, and it did not. The flies departed, but the slaves remained.

No sooner had the Egyptians breathed a united sigh of relief for the freedom from flies, than they woke to a plague of boils. Their bodies were covered with them—great blisters that itched and burst and became infected. Doctors were unable to treat the blains because they themselves were so badly troubled by them. No one was out in the streets and no work was done; all that could be heard was children crying miserably and the moans of the afflicted.

"Rameses, relent! Don't go back on it this time. Believe me, *believe me,* this plague, as bad as it is, is not the worst that can happen! Don't you see now that this is God's doing?"

"My priests say it is the fault of a volcanic eruption across the Big Sea. The ash cloud is blowing toward us and that's what's causing the disturbances in the order of nature."

"So at least those two old conjurers are not pretending they can bring about such wonders, as they did about the blood?"

Rameses rose from his throne in a fury.

"Get out of my sight! I never want to set eyes on another of you accursed Hebrews in my life!"

This time Moses was more cautious. He went to Aaron and Miriam.

"He says he will let us go. Perhaps if—if I didn't mention to God that He should withdraw the plague of boils until we're well on our way—?"

Miriam said, "Moses, God knows everything. How can you talk of deceiving Him?"

Aaron said, "Try it."

But Miriam was right. The boils dried up miraculously overnight. The people rejoiced, blessed Pharaoh and his priests, paid homage to their gods. And Pharaoh sent word to his overseers to work the slaves as they had never worked before.

"I want my tomb finished! Not a man is to rest more than one hour in eight until it is done."

More slaves than ever were collapsing from exhaustion; an average of three a day were dying as they chipped and hacked into the sides of the great stone hillside where Rameses' tomb was being carved into solid rock. They were hauled out and flung into death-pits they had already dug themselves. Moses wrung his hands and wept with anguish.

"Why is Rameses doing this? There will be another plague."

"I hope so," said Aaron grimly.

He had his wish. That evening the cattle of Egypt began to die.

No one could recognize the disease, no one could

do anything. The cows staggered and threw back their heads, fell to their knees, and in less than an hour, they were dead. Hundreds and hundreds of them—whole herds. Farmers formed delegations and besieged the palace. The guards tried to keep them back and wounded several with their spears, but the farmers were frantic, watching their wealth die with their beasts.

Moses saw his moment and, without waiting to be summoned, came before the Pharaoh.

"Rameses, stop. Stop! I implore you, open your eyes and see the truth. Spare your people, stop this pointless agony! Let my people go, in God's name!"

"The fallout from the volcano is killing the cattle," growled Rameses. "Hotep says so. They are choking on the ash."

"*What ash?* I see no ash. It's a miracle. Why can't you realize it?"

Rameses, hearing the racket of the protesting farmers outside his windows, brooded.

"Very well, I will let them go."

"Can I believe you?"

"When the cattle stop dying, you can go. You have my word, given on the feather of Maat." This was a strong oath, and Moses let himself hope.

The death of the cattle came to an end when

practically every cow in Egypt lay dead. But again Pharaoh broke his word.

Though the Hebrews had not directly suffered from the plagues so far, Moses by now pitied the Egyptians, and was terrified of what would happen next.

What happened was hail.

The cloud that covered the city, quite out of season, was not an ash cloud as the priests kept saying. It opened and out of it poured lumps of ice as big as fists. If a man was struck on the head by one, it could kill him. Again the people of Egypt were confined to their houses. But the houses themselves were not safe. The pounding of the hail on the flat roofs could break them. Crops were beaten flat. Roads were churned up and made impassable by heaps of ice. It was suicide to leave shelter. Work on the tomb was suspended—the entrance to it was blocked by ice.

Even the palace was badly damaged. Rameses grew cunning.

"All right, I will make you an offer. Take your people into the desert and sacrifice to your god, as you wanted. But bring them back."

"That you call freedom?"

Rameses threw out his hands. "Moses, be reasonable. I need them. I can't run the country without them."

"And yet you give them no respect, no dignity. You have them driven, flogged, and killed. Is this the way to repay sweated labor that holds up your whole society?"

Rameses stared at him, wrestling with this strange concept.

"I don't have to give respect and dignity to beasts I own. That's all the slaves are."

Moses turned away in despair.

The hail stopped. The sun came out. The ice melted and everything steamed and streamed with water, and was mired in mud. But the land dried up quickly and the farmers began to take stock.

The wheat and maize crops were totally destroyed, but the second crop of barley was only just showing above the ground and had not done so badly. Its promising green was increasing every day in the sun; there was hope yet of a good harvest. The fruit trees, too, had not suffered too much—only the top branches had been damaged. The tough date palms had withstood the storm very well. Perhaps something could be saved after all.

And then one morning the farmers in their fields heard a faint, faraway droning sound. They looked up, and from the other side of the river they saw a dark cloud approaching.

The younger men stood gaping at the cloud,

wondering what it could be. The older ones knew too well, and with dread in their hearts they threw down their implements and ran for home, there to rage and revile their gods. They knew that all was lost.

In half an hour the first locusts bumped and tumbled down on the ground and began to eat everything in sight. The trees were completely covered with them, and were stripped bare in minutes. The emerald of the barley fields turned to brown as the creatures descended on them in millions and began to eat the young shoots down to ground-level. Even the broken remains of the ruined crops were not spared.

The younger farmers fought in a frenzy. They stamped, and beat the locusts with their hoes, they banged on pots and shouted themselves hoarse to drive them away. They called to their families to come and help them dig trenches, shovel the locusts in, and bury them. They even tried to burn them. They destroyed thousands of them, but there were always more. It was hopeless—in a single day, the locusts ensured that next winter there would be critical shortages throughout the land.

This time when the farmers marched on the palace, people from the city joined them. They would all be hungry together; there was no distinction now between rich and poor, farmer and merchant, young and old. The entire population was at the gates, shouting, screaming, beseeching, wailing. Rameses stood hidden and looked down on the seething mass of his people and thought he was beaten.

Moses came when he was sent for. He didn't grovel and beg any more. He stood stern and tall and said, "Are you ready now?"

Rameses tried one last ploy.

"Huy and Hotep say they've got rid of the locusts."

"Yes indeed, they have all gone. Remarkable."

"Why are you sarcastic?"

"Really, those old foxes are too absurd. Of course the locusts have gone, there is nothing left to eat. But they have laid their eggs, which will hatch, and the hatchlings will go for the stored grain."

Rameses paled. The vast grain stores were all that stood between Egypt and famine. "They can't get at that!"

"They can do what God lets them do. Only a miracle will save the people from starvation. And you know what will make that miracle happen."

Rameses was silent. He had not been able to eat or sleep properly for weeks. He was desperately wor-

ried; his little son had begun to ask him about the
plagues and he had no answer. Now the whole citi-
zenry was at his gates and he did not know what to
do. He played for time.

"Is this god of yours really doing all this?"

"Yes."

"He must be very angry with me," he said whim-
sically.

"Don't make jokes, Rameses. This is no time for
levity. The worst is yet to come."

"Worse than starvation staring us in the face?"

"Yes. Much worse."

"What, for instance?"

Moses gazed at him. The words came from elsewhere—not from him. "It will be the worst thing you
can imagine."

"Moses. You're still my brother. Can't you reason
with your god? Can't you explain that he is asking the
impossible?"

"If only you had treated the Hebrews better, God
wouldn't be so angry. And the people would never
have believed me or followed me."

Rameses sprawled back on his throne. "We have
yet to see if they will—follow you. Yes. I would like
to see one man lead so many thousand people out of
their homes, away from their generous allotment of

bread and beer, and into a pitiless wilderness where it is *they* who will starve. What will you do when they are crying for food?"

"God will provide for them."

"In the desert? I don't think so."

"Don't concern yourself. All you need do is let them go."

Rameses made a lazy gesture, but with a hand that trembled. "Go on then. Take them."

"You've said it so often."

"I mean it this time. I've had enough. I'm convinced. You've won." But his face wore a cynical, crafty smile.

Moses started out of the room. Behind him, Rameses drawled:

"Oh, you might ask your god to kill off all the locust eggs, will you?"

Moses went back to Miriam and Aaron, and said, "Not yet. It won't happen yet. He says he believes, but he doesn't—he'll go back on it. I don't know why. I'm afraid the worst must happen before we can leave." He put his head in his hands. All he could feel was dread for what was to come.

CHAPTER 15

THE NINTH
PLAGUE

A great darkness descended over the Land of
Egypt. It was a darkness that was more than an
absence of light. It had a thickness, a weight.
It pressed down on the city like something solid. The
little lights of torches and lamps seemed hardly able
to penetrate it, lighting only what was immediately
around them.

No one moaned or wailed now. No one came to
the palace gates to complain. They were too frightened, too oppressed. The silence of a great fear hung
over the whole country. Or perhaps, thought Moses,
huddled in the home of Aaron and Miriam in
Goshen, sound could not travel through this blanket
of perpetual night.

Three terrible days passed, days when it seemed
to the Egyptians that the sun-god hid his face as if
knowing that his power had been overtaken.

Moses said to Miriam, "Do you think this is

the worst plague, the one I've been dreading?"

"Whatever God does will be right," said Miriam.

Moses, with a heavy heart, counted the plagues—blood, frogs, lice, flies, boils, cattle-bane, hail, locusts, and now, darkness. But it was not their number or severity that counted, it was that none of them had brought about the Hebrews' freedom. Surely there would be another, more terrible than all the rest.

"I must go and plead with him once more," said Moses, rising wearily. "Perhaps he is ready to relent."

"Take a torch and walk with care," said Tzipporah.

When Moses left Goshen and entered the Egyptian city, it was like walking into a thick, black mist, but with more substance than mist—almost, it seemed, he must push through. The torch lit no more than two cubits around itself. Moses made his way slowly and cautiously to the palace.

There were no guards outside the gate, no slaves within to prostrate themselves or bar the way to Pharaoh. They had all fled the terrible darkness. Moses called: "Rameses! Rameses!" His voice did not echo in the great stone halls and corridors, but was muffled.

Pharaoh was not in his private apartments. Moses came at last to the great throne room where Seti used to summon them. There was a mighty statue of the old Pharaoh here now, put up after his death, and it was from this that Rameses at last answered Moses' calls.

"I'm here, Brother."

His voice was slurred. Moses raised his torch. Rameses was seated, as it were, in his father's lap, cradling a goblet of wine.

"What do you want? Wait, let me guess. Could you intend asking me some slight favor, such as letting your people go?"

"Rameses, we must bring this to an end. Before it's too late."

"Before it's too late," Rameses repeated drunkenly. "You don't call this too late?" He gestured around him at the inky darkness.

"This is not the worst."

Rameses sent his cup crashing to the floor and shouted: "I am sick of your threats of doom! What could be worse than what we've endured so far? I hate your god! I will not obey him! I am a god myself, why should I yield to him, strong though he is?"

"So you acknowledge His power?"

"Yes yes yes! My gods have failed me. I have sent those two idiots, Huy and Hotep, packing. I should have done it years ago."

"Can we talk? I'll come up to you. It will be like

the old days, when we climbed into the lap of Horus to hide from the priests."

"No! Don't come up. This is *my* father's statue," Rameses said childishly. "I don't want to talk to you."

"Please, Rameses! Can't we recover a little of our closeness?"

"You want to talk about yet another plague!"

"No. About you and me."

There was a pause, and then the sound of sandals on stone as Rameses slid down to the floor. He looked at Moses for a moment through the gloom.

"Talk, then," he said sullenly.

Moses searched his mind for something to bridge the years.

"Remember how we changed the heads of the gods, when we were young?" said Moses.

A drunken grin twitched at the corners of Rameses' mouth. "You put the hippo's head on the crocodile, the crocodile's on the falcon."

"You did that. I didn't."

"Whoever did it, Huy and Hotep thought it was some terrible omen and fasted for two months. Father was furious! You were always getting me into trouble. But then . . . in those days, you were always able to get me out of it." His voice, wine-soaked, took on a whining tone. "You're trying to wheedle me, to bring back our childhood. Do you think I don't wish things could be as they were? But—"

"Father . . . it's so dark. I'm frightened," said a little voice out of the blackness.

Both men turned. Into the constricted glow of the torchlight crept the small figure of Rameses' son. He was holding a tiny clay lamp; the flame on its wick barely lit his face.

"Every time I open my eyes I think I've gone blind."

Rameses sat on the floor against the statue and pulled the boy down between his knees. "And you lit your lamp yourself and found your way here through the dark?" The boy nodded solemnly, but tears glistened in his eyes. "Brave lad! You will make a great pharaoh when your time comes. You will not be a weak link, will you?"

"What's a weak link, Father?"

"It's what my father warned me not to be. Remember when we went to watch the tug-of-war across the canal, and all the men were strong and pulled hard except one, who let the rope go and fell back on his fellows so that they all went tumbling—"

"—and the ones in front were all pulled into the water! Yes!" the boy said, and almost laughed, but the fear was too strong on him.

"That man who let go, and whom I afterwards

had flogged, was the weak link," said Rameses.

"Is *he* a weak link?" asked the boy suddenly, pointing to Moses.

Rameses looked at Moses for a long time.

"He is not a link at all," he said. "He is a breaker of links. Do you want to know who he is? He is the man who is causing all these bad things to happen."

The boy cowered against his father. "Why is he here? Will he make more bad things happen?"

"He says he will."

"Rameses," said Moses. "Don't tell the boy lies. I am not causing all this. You are, with your stubbornness."

"I will not be given orders. Am I not Pharaoh?"

The boy did laugh now, and clapped his hands. "Answer that, bad man!" he crowed.

Moses looked at the little bright-eyed boy with the lock of royalty on the side of his head, and words he had not thought of saying sprang to his mouth. "Pity the children," he said under his breath.

"What?"

"The children, Rameses. The beautiful, innocent children. Our father had no pity on them. Show that you are something better!" The two men stared at each other through the gloom. Suddenly Moses let out a cry as if stabbed.

Rameses jumped up. "What? What is it?"

"Something is coming—something terrible!" He staggered as if he had received a mighty push, then righted himself with an effort. "Rameses!" he cried, with the utmost urgency. "You once said to me— remember, when I killed the overseer—that you could make it as if it never happened. Now you have the power to stop something from happening. Do it, I'm begging you—relent! Or there will be such a cry over all Egypt that has never been equaled!" He held out his hands as if to keep off some nameless terror.

Rameses, holding his son's hand, leaned against the base of his father's statue and stared at Moses with unrelenting eyes.

"Your people," he said, "have been nothing but trouble. My father had the right idea about how to deal with them. I have followed him in so many ways. Perhaps I will follow him in this, also."

His eyes went to the painting on the wall.

Moses lifted his head, speechless with horror. He knew God was listening. He knew God had been waiting for this—the last, heartless threat. It was all Moses could do not to leap forward to force the words back into Rameses' mouth.

Instead he almost ran from the room, the name-less dread like the storm-wind he had foreseen beside the Nile seeming to drive him from his brother's side. But he couldn't help hearing a little voice behind him, puzzled and questioning:

"Father? Father?"

CHAPTER 16

THE ANGEL
OF
DEATH

When Moses started back to Goshen, his mind was in ferment. He was sweating and trembling, unable to think for terror and distress. But during the walk, he was given the gift of calm. And God spoke to him.

Aaron, Miriam, and Tzipporah were waiting for him.

"The end is coming," he told them. "Gather the people, I must tell them what I know."

Within an hour, the heads of households were crowded into the open space beside the main well. Moses stepped onto the wellhead and waited for silence. Then he addressed the vast crowd in a loud voice.

"You are to take each of you a lamb, a lamb without blemish in its first year, and kill it, and with its blood, mark your lintels and doorposts. Tonight the Angel of Death will visit the Land of Egypt, but

when He sees the blood upon our door frames He
will pass over us.

"Tonight we eat the meal that shall be called the
Feast of the Passover, and it is to be exactly as I tell
you, for God is precise. You will roast and eat the
lambs whose blood marked your lintels. You will pick
bitter herbs and eat them in memory of the bitterness
of your enslavement. You will crush the root that is
hot in the mouth and mix it to paste—let it stand for
your sufferings as you mixed the mortar to bind the
bricks.

"And you will make bread-dough, but you shall
put no leaven in it—there will be no time for it to
rise. Bake some and pack some up, to take with you
on the journey. Don't sit down to eat. Eat where you
stand, every man with his sandals on his feet and his
staff in his hand, ready to leave at a moment's notice."

The awe-stricken men hurried to obey him. By
the light of torches they chose and slaughtered the
lambs, and the women daubed the openings to their
homes with blood, making a red splash.

"But will the Angel of Death be able to see the
marks?" they whispered.

"Have faith," urged Miriam as she moved from
house to house. "We must have faith." Her whole
mind was afire with a passionate, and wholly posi-

tive, belief that God was great, loving, and merciful, that He was on their side, that in sparing them whatever fate He had in store for their persecutors, He would prove Himself for all ages to come to be their God and they His people. She had no room in her exalted thoughts for pain or punishment, or for the Egyptians either.

Moses felt strengthened. These people, enslaved so long, were a strong and obedient people after all. But as midnight came a cold feeling of horror swept over him like an icy mist. He ate little of the passover meal. Heavy with dread of what was happening close by, he spent the rest of the night in prayer.

What happened in the Egyptian city they never knew, for who sees the Angel of Death at his work? All the Hebrews knew was that as dawn broke—and it broke for Egypt, too, the darkness having lifted to give place to a deeper darkness—came first the stunned silence of discovery, and then a moan, and then a terrible, universal cry that seemed to reach to the unheeding heavens.

Not a household had escaped. From the humblest peasant's hut to the Pharaoh's palace itself, the firstborn of every family, male and female, had been struck down.

Some as they lay asleep. Some as they went to draw water. Some in the act of eating or drinking. Some as they tended their flocks. Some as they said their prayers, as they loved, or laughed, or talked, or cried in the night. In the midst of their dreams, their anger, their affections, their appetites, their idle thoughts, their midnight tasks, *they were*—and then in the blink of an eye, *they were not.* Death struck them and they ended, the speech still in their mouths, the food in their hands, the secret feelings in their hearts. In the midst of their sin or their good deeds, bowing to their gods or lying in their mother's arms, cursing their fates or thinking hopefully about the day to come—the Angel of Death impartially snatched them from themselves and went his way, leaving behind him empty bodies, and bottomless grief.

Through the stricken city, Moses sought his brother for the last time.

He had learned at dawn what had overtaken the city. It confirmed his worst fears, and he was filled with a sense of mourning. He knew what he would find when he found Rameses, and he prepared himself as well as he could, borne up by Miriam's words: "Whatever God does is right." But he could not help thinking about the innocent child, and the thought escaped him, "Our God can indeed be wrathful."

Rameses was in the palace temple. He stood beside a stone altar with the body of his son in his arms. Moses stopped. That boy who had jumped about crying, "Our gods are better!" had his answer now. Yet—oh, yet, he had been so *alive*! Moses could not quite believe that some exception had not been made, that that sturdy, lively little lad, descendent of a hundred kings, was no more. Who would be the next Pharaoh now?

Rameses laid the child on the altar and drew a linen sheet over him. Before he covered the face, he touched its forehead with his own. Then he straightened up and spoke to Moses. It was as if a corpse spoke.

"You and your people have my permission to go."

Moses reached toward him in pity, but Rameses became taut in every muscle. "Leave me!" he said.

Moses saw the awful hatred in his eyes and turned away, heartsick.

He fled from the place where he had grown up as a prince of Egypt, but before he had taken twenty steps it was as if his very heart's blood turned to tears. He leaned against a wall and wept for all the sorrowing parents, and for the dead children who had paid the price of slavery and defiance of God's commands. For long minutes he wept with selfless grief, not least for Rameses, knowing that within, his one-time brother wept too. He had claimed godhood, but he was only a man, after all—to whom could he turn now for comfort? To stone idols? In that crisis, Moses finally and forever cast out the gods of his childhood.

In Goshen they were all waiting for him, a great crowd. They were clutching their children to them as if they would never let them go.

Miriam came running to meet him. "What now? We are ready!"

"It is time to go."

A great cry of joy and release went up all around him and was taken up by thousands of voices. "Moses!" the people cried. "Moses, our redeemer!" But Moses knew that he had only achieved the first goal. The greatest—to get them safely to their destination—lay ahead.

And as he helped Tzipporah to load the beasts of burden, he thought of Rameses' hate-filled eyes, and wondered, "He has lost the thing that was dearest to him, and now he is losing us—the means to fulfill his grand ambitions. What more can God do to him, if he changes his mind yet again?"

FREEDOM BEGINS

T he slaves, who were slaves no more, with one accord left their miserable dwellings and set off with Moses in the lead—a long, long caravan of men and women, children and animals, winding out of the city, traveling east. No one tried to stop them.

It was the longed-for first day of freedom. They were all so joyful that none of them gave a thought to the dangers and hardships that might lie ahead. The children skipped and played; the women sang (Miriam, who had a gift for music, made up a joyous freedom song and they all took it up) and walked arm-in-arm with their neighbors. The men shouted encouragement to each other and strode along, feeling new strength in their work-worn limbs.

Even the sheep and goats and donkeys were frisky, trotting out of the line to snatch at bits of fodder; the children ran out to drive them back, and

then fell to playing in the sand. But no one became impatient or angry.

Occasionally someone irresistibly looked back, but the cloud of dust that rose behind them prevented them seeing what they had left. "Egypt is no more," they said. "It is nothing to us now! Only what lies ahead matters!"

At noon they ate and drank heartily from their store. Those who had brought beer passed it around and they savored their happiness.

That night they made camp on the dry ground. They combined what fuel they had and made a few large fires, and drew lots whose goats should be slaughtered and roasted for everyone. When the fires burned out, it was cold, but no one complained. Moses basked in pride. A hardy people, ready for anything!

But before many days had passed, food became a problem. "When will God feed us?" Moses was asked, when a system of rationing had been introduced by Aaron.

"We must prove ourselves worthy," he answered.

Aaron, now wholly with Moses and staunch in belief, told the men to make bows and spears, and sent hunting parties ahead to look for game. But the

Hebrews were used to having their food given to them by their Egyptian taskmasters. The hunters drifted back to the main party baffled and empty-handed. Some of them had gotten lost altogether, and search parties had to be sent to look for them. They had never learned to orient themselves by reading the heavens.

The water was running out. A subdued murmuring began to reach Moses' ears.

"This is going to be a hungry march unless God helps us. Where is the first well? Are there oases up ahead?"

Moses had no idea. Tzipporah, looking at the vast throng of people and beasts, wondered if she should tell Moses to lead them toward her people's camping grounds. But she blenched when she thought of how quickly such a mighty thirst would drink the Midian wells dry. She decided to say nothing. God had brought them here. Let God solve their problems.

Miriam, for all her faith, was practical. "God helps those who help themselves. Set out pots at night and spread hides above them to catch dew."

Day after day, the vast caravan tramped on.

No one sang or danced or shouted cheerfully now. It took energy enough to keep going. Many of the children had to be carried. Sandals began to break, animals to stray, burdens to become so heavy it was tempting to leave them behind. Moses, Aaron, and Miriam were not in the lead now; they moved back and forth among the people, encouraging, carrying, helping, keeping up their spirits, and Tzipporah helped them.

Moses was beginning to be very seriously worried. Had God abandoned him? Miriam's shining, unwavering faith kept his heart up. He sat with her every night, talking things over, borrowing her courage. Tzipporah watched. It was hard for her, but she made up her mind not to be hurt that he turned to his sister more than to her. She must be as strong now in mind and spirit as she was in body. She must accept that Moses was not only hers now— he belonged to the people. Homesick though she was, and desperately missing her children, she was resolved: as long as Moses needed her, as long as he clung to her in the nights, she would be his little bird; she would nest in his heart and not fly away.

One morning after many days, when they woke from their cold night's rest, Moses, who as always had woken early and climbed to a ridge to watch the dawn, let out a shout and beckoned.

Those who were awake surged up behind him and stood in a long line, staring down. They had reached the crest of some hills, and far below lay a desert valley. In its midst was a body of blue water, stretching away to north and south, its eastern shore lost in the morning mist.

"What is it? Is it the Big Sea?"

"No, that lies to the north. This is another sea. I heard of it when I was with the Midianites. It's the border of Egypt."

Those nearest stared at him. "Are we still in Egypt?"

"Egypt is vast. It's not just the city."

"It must be the whole world!" said one of the children.

Moses bent to lift her up. "No, *biti*. Beyond that sea down there is the Wilderness of Sinai, and beyond that is the land we're going to, our own land that God has promised us."

"The land of milk and honey?"

"Yes."

"But how shall we cross the sea?"

Moses gazed downward. How, indeed?

"I don't know yet," he said, trying to keep his voice calm and confident. "We shall see when we reach it."

The people were excited. They packed up quickly and began the downhill march onto the untrodden sand dunes that bordered the sea. When, after some hours, they had left the rocky hills behind, they felt the coolness off the water blowing into their faces and they began to hurry. In the end they ran, pell-mell, like thirsty cattle to the water's edge. There, perforce, they stopped.

"What shall we do now?" asked a great swell of voices. "How shall we cross?"

Moses felt thousands of pairs of eyes fixed on him, thousands of pairs of ears waiting for his answer. He stood still and silent. His heart turned the question upon God. "What shall we do now, Lord? How shall we cross?"

Across all the mighty throng of people, there was not a sound. They were waiting and straining their ears. And that was how they all heard it at the same moment, though their feet knew it first: a vibrating. A trembling in the sand under them.

They looked at each other, merely uneasy at first, and then, as the sound came, the blood fled from their faces. They clutched each other, and every head turned back the way they had come.

The sound was many noises put together, very

faint at first, but growing every minute. It was not long before each contributing sound could be distinctly heard: the drumming of hooves on stones. The snorting and neighing of horses. The clatter of wheels. The cries of men. The crack of whips.

The crowd seemed to shrink in upon itself. There were gasps, groans, and screams. And then, over the crest of the hills, still far away but clearly visible, they came: the plumed helmets, the glittering shields, the galloping horses, the bronze spearheads catching the sun. Pharaoh's hosts, led by Pharaoh himself, proud as the sun-god all in gold, dazzling to the eye and terrifying to the heart.

The next moment, the Hebrews fell upon Moses, almost pushing him backwards into the sea.

"What have you done to us? We're trapped! Were there no graves for us in Egypt that you brought us here to die in the desert? At least as slaves we were safe!"

Moses could scarcely think above the racket, but their words shook him to the core. It was Aaron, at his side, who shouted: "Why are you so frightened? Trust God!"—at the top of his lungs. Those nearest fell back a little, ashamed, but still terrified.

"But look! Pharaoh's coming after us! He will take us back!"

"Isn't that what you want? Don't you want to be slaves again?" cried Moses, furious at their feebleness.

They fell silent. The oncoming army with its chariots and horsemen was now in clear sight, racing toward them down the distant hillside. Soon, soon, they would catch up with them. In an hour, they might all be slaughtered, or if it was the Pharaoh's will, taken prisoner and marched back to punishment. What choice did they have but to trust God, after all?

But the sea at their backs! The deep, impassable, boatless sea!

Suddenly their ears were caught by a noise that drowned out everything, even the thudding of their frightened hearts.

They turned toward it. The seawater was boiling! And out of it burst a great pillar of cloudy fire that whirled and flew over the heads of the vast throng, so close that they cried out and fell on their faces in a swathe as if a great scythe had cut them down.

The pillar moved swiftly across the sand and planted itself in fiery splendor before Pharaoh's chariot, forcing it to halt. The troops, mounted or in chariots behind it, dragged on their reins. The horses reared up in terror, and all was confusion—the clashing of wheels bumping together and men shouting to each other and a snapping of spears as the ranks were broken.

But the pillar of fire did not move to overwhelm them, and Pharaoh regained his courage. He stood tall in his chariot and shouted back:

"It is a desert whirlwind, nothing worse! Officers, regroup the chariots! When it withdraws, we will move upon the slaves, we will take them all, and there shall be rich rewards for every man of you who stands to his duty!"

The men were trained to obedience and responded to strong leadership. Though each one of them could see this was no mere wind, for the pillar was shot through with fire, they had no choice but to get control of their horses and recover their ranks. The promise of reward helped.

Far below, Moses stood facing the sea and turned his eyes expectantly up toward God. And now came an answer.

"Moses, with my staff thou shalt do my wonders."

Moses felt his doubts and fears dry up in him like dew in the sun. He stood squarely facing the expanse of water, sensing the press of panic-stricken people on three sides. He seized his staff in both hands and boldly struck the water with it, crying out: "Let us pass!"

And the sea parted.

It was surely the most miraculous sight that had ever been witnessed in the world. The huge body of water split asunder and reared up on two sides, forming two great walls reaching as high as the hills the Hebrews had just crossed. Water, clear and turquoise blue, topped by two long motionless waves, without splash or spume, poised, towering, held as steady as canyon walls. Walls that appeared as glass, but were yet soft yielding water, needing to flow and fall but obeying the will of God to stay upright against every law of water's nature.

Between the walls was a broad pathway across the bed of the sea.

When the people saw this greatest of wonders, they fell back in their thousands, some upon the ground, their legs unable to hold them. Not a cry passed their lips, for they were awe-stricken, stunned. And then, as Moses began to shout to them: "Forward! Go through! Hurry! Hurry!" they began to come to themselves.

But they were terrified to enter the pathway between the sea walls. They seemed paralyzed with awe.

"Go! Go, will you, go!" Moses kept screaming at them. They edged forward but stopped dead on the shore as if another wall, an invisible one, stood in their way.

"How can it stay up? It will fall on us!" they breathed to each other.

Then Aaron stepped in front of them. "My friends, we are in God's hands. Follow me, and don't be afraid." And he walked boldly between the towering walls of water.

The people stared. Moses, exasperated beyond bearing, shouted: "Have I saved so many disbelieving cowards? Miriam! Help me! We have no time! *Make* them go!"

And now in desperation he began to push and drag them. This the men who had been slaves responded to. Slowly the whole cavalcade began first to creep, then to walk very slowly, and finally, with the fear of Pharaoh urging them on, to run and stumble between the walls of the sea.

CHAPTER 18

OUT
OF THE
DEPTHS

iriam, who was marching ahead, heard them coming, looked over her shoulder—and jumped aside just in time.

The people were in tumult. From being paralyzed by fear, they were now galvanized, and once started they were like a flash flood in a desert wadi. They rushed past her helter-skelter, panting and gasping, stumbling, being dragged along by their loved ones, the herds stampeding beside them, bleating with terror.

She saw a child go down near her and hurled herself into the crowd, dragging the child clear just before it was trampled on. Before she could think what to do, a wild-eyed mother escaped the flow, turned back, snatched the child from Miriam's arms and fled on.

There were stones and boulders strewn on what had been the sea bottom, impediments that were breaking the wheels of handcarts and causing people and animals to stumble. Miriam found a big rock near the water-wall and climbed onto it. Ahead, she could see Aaron beginning to run lest the crowd behind should overwhelm him. Behind she could see Moses trying to control the surge of people. They must be slowed, Miriam thought, or some would be killed in the rush.

Moses suddenly rode past her on to the back of his terrified camel. Miriam shouted to him: "Moses! Lead them! Slow them down!" She saw him manage to overtake the crowd. Some distance from the men in front, he caught up with Aaron, turned the camel sideways and held out his staff. The first men braced themselves against the press behind and gradually slowed the whole crowd to a controllable pace. Moses dismounted, and, holding his staff high, led them on.

Miriam stood on her rock as the Hebrews passed her in a blur of faces. She leaned back, then jerked forward again. The water-wall—it had soaked her shoulders and hair! Irresistibly curious, she thrust her arm into it. Yes, it was water, salt water, and there were fish swimming in it! She smiled in ecstacy and whispered, "Hear me, O God! There is none like You!"

She stopped worrying about the crush, or the threat of Pharaoh's chariots. As Tzipporah passed her, half-carrying an old woman, Miriam slipped like an eel into the crowd to help her. In her head was forming a song of praise, and she felt heart-free, fear-free enough to try it over as she hurried along. All would be well! Who could doubt it now?

On the western bank, the pillar of fire disappeared, and Pharaoh, waving his troops on exultantly, looked ahead, and saw what his eyes did not believe.

All his men saw it, too. Yet they dared not admit, even to themselves, that they had seen it. They refused to see the miracle. They saw their Pharaoh, his whip-arm raised to signal them on, racing unchecked across the sand toward the sea-that-was-not-a-sea, but a roadway, wide enough to take five chariots abreast. The last of the fleeing Hebrews were still in sight—the soldiers' quarry, the source of their prosperity, the spur to their ambitions. Their officers' rallying cry before they set off from the city still rang in their ears:

"The wretched slaves have escaped to the last man, and Pharaoh says, if we don't recapture them and bring them back, *we* will have to take their places! Into the brickfields and under the lash with him who is last in the chase!"

So they rode their chariots and lashed their

horses between the towering sea-walls and never even glanced at them, nor felt the overwhelming power that held them upright. They had lost sight of their leader, but they no longer needed him. The excitement of the chase and the nearness of success drove them blindly on.

Rameses had fallen.

Just as he was about to enter the unnatural blue-green canyon, one of his horses, with an animal's sense of the uncanny, came to a dead stop. The other tried to race on and was violently checked, slewing the chariot and breaking the central shaft. The chariot pitched off its wheels, and Rameses half jumped and was half catapulted into the air.

He landed as he had been trained, hands first, then, head tucked under, on his shoulders, and rolled for a long way down a dune. His helmet came off, his sword was lost. He reached the bottom and lay stunned for long moments, then jumped to his feet.

He was in a dip and could see nothing. Straining every muscle, he ran back up the slope through clinging sand. From the crest of the dune, he turned and surveyed the scene.

The air was crystal-clear now. In the remote distance he could see the far shore of the sea, with a clotted dark mass on it which was the Hebrews. All of them. Even as he looked, the last trickle flowed out of the sea path and up the other side.

But before the thought "I'll recover them yet!" had cleared his brain, he saw something so terrible that his mind and body were seized in a grip akin to the grip of death.

His soldiers—the cream of his standing army, six hundred men, their weapons, chariots and horses— were all charging between the sea walls, riding full-tilt after their quarry. But the motionless crests of the long waves at the top of the walls were not perfectly still any more. They were coming to life.

Rameses watched in helpless horror as they curled slowly and gracefully inward, one toward the other. The walls seemed to *awaken*. From standing rigid, they swayed, bulged, buckled. And as the crests of the waves met, forming a tunnel as tall as the tallest temple, the water remembered itself. It remembered its nature. No longer upheld by God, it crashed, and with a roar like a mighty wind, sought its own level.

And Pharaoh's men and his horses and his chariots, together with all his hopes of vengeance, were drowned in the depths of the sea.

As Rameses stood there and watched, the tempest of spray that drenched him seemed to wash the scales from his eyes. Moses' God lifted the pharaoh's blindness and removed the hardness from his heart, so that he might recognize at last God's terrible power, and feel the devastation of total defeat.

Moses climbed at the head of the column to the top of a high bank on the eastern shore. At his side, Miriam sang.

She had found, somehow, somewhere, a little drum, and she beat it with her fingers in a frenzy of joy. Her song of praise and triumph was taken up by a few voices and then by many. It spread over the whole assembly until every voice was raised in God's praise.

"We will sing a song to our God,
We will exalt him!
He has come to our aid.
Horse and rider He has overthrown.
Who is like unto You, O Lord?
Indeed, there is no God like ours!"

Moses, with Tzipporah and Aaron beside him, ushered the people past him. They were the last to go over the top of the hill that would hide the sea from their sight. They paused and looked back.

Far away in the sunlight, beyond the water, a tiny flash of reflected light caught Moses' eye.

Could it be? Could Rameses have survived, and be standing on the far shore, looking as Moses was looking—remembering, as he was?

Moses stared and stared. He could feel nothing but a sort of fading sadness. He turned to Aaron.

"Now I have no brother but you."

He put his arm around Aaron's shoulders.

Tzipporah was looking the other way, out over the great mass of people, still singing Miriam's song with a power and beauty that seemed supernatural. It was as if God accepted their song-offering, drew it up, and used it to fill the heavens.

"Look, Moses. Look at your people," she said. "They are free."

And they walked down the hill together after those who would come to be called the Children of Israel.

LYNNE REID BANKS is the highly acclaimed author of more than thirty books, twenty of them for young readers, as well as a number of plays. She is best known for the enormously popular series of novels about a boy whose toy Indian comes to life, beginning with *The Indian in the Cupboard*. A *New York Times* Best Book of the Year and the winner of numerous state awards, it was made into a full-length feature film in 1995. Her many other titles include *One More River, Broken Bridge, Harry the Poisonous Centipede, Angela and Diabola,* and *Maura's Angel.* Ms. Banks lives in Dorset, England, with her sculptor husband, Chaim Stephenson.